THE PRINCESS AND THE BRIGAND

"What you are saying," Vladilas said, "is that you are waiting until the King, your father, is dead, when you intend to take over the throne."

In a cold voice, she managed to reply: "That, General, is my business!"

"It also happens to be mine!"

"Yours?"

"Yes, mine!" he said quietly. "And this is where you have a choice. You can marry me and I will ensure the defence of Zokāla—or else I will take over the country!"

BRIDE TO A BRIGAND

A Camfield Novel of Love

Camfield Place,
Hatfield
Hertfordshire,
England

Dearest Reader,

This starts a new and very exciting era of my books with Jove. They already have nearly two hundred of my books which they have had ever since they became the first publisher to bring out my books in America. Now all my paperbacks in future will be published by them.

As you already know, Camfield Place in Hertfordshire is my home, which originally existed in 1275, but was rebuilt in 1867 by the grandfather of Beatrix Potter.

It was here in this lovely house, with the best view of the county, that she wrote *The Tale of Peter Rabbit*. Mr. McGregor's garden is exactly as she described it. The door in the wall that the fat little rabbit could not squeeze underneath and the goldfish pool where the white cat sat twitching its tail are still there.

I had Camfield Place blessed when I came here in 1950 and was so happy with my husband until he died, and now with my children and grandchildren, that I know the atmosphere is filled with love and we have all been very lucky.

It is easy here to write of love and I feel you will enjoy the new Camfield Novels of Love, which are a little different from those that you have read before. The plots are definitely more exciting and the covers more romantic. They come to you, like all my novels, with love.

Bless you,

Books by Barbara Cartland

THE ADVENTURER
AGAIN THIS RAPTURE
ARMOUR AGAINST
  LOVE
THE AUDACIOUS
  ADVENTURESS
BARBARA CARTLAND'S
  BOOK OF BEAUTY
  AND HEALTH
THE BITTER WINDS OF
  LOVE
BLUE HEATHER
BROKEN BARRIERS
THE CAPTIVE HEART
THE COIN OF LOVE
THE COMPLACENT WIFE
COUNT THE STARS
CUPID RIDES PILLION
DANCE ON MY HEART
DESIRE OF THE HEART
DESPERATE DEFIANCE
THE DREAM WITHIN
A DUEL OF HEARTS
ELIZABETH EMPRESS OF
  AUSTRIA
ELIZABETHAN LOVER
THE ENCHANTED
  MOMENT
THE ENCHANTED
  WALTZ
THE ENCHANTING EVIL
ESCAPE FROM PASSION
FOR ALL ETERNITY
A GHOST IN MONTE
  CARLO
THE GOLDEN GONDOLA
A HALO FOR THE DEVIL
A HAZARD OF HEARTS
A HEART IS BROKEN
THE HEART OF THE
  CLAN
THE HIDDEN EVIL
THE HIDDEN HEART
THE HORIZONS OF LOVE

AN INNOCENT IN
  MAYFAIR
IN THE ARMS OF LOVE
THE IRRESISTIBLE BUCK
JOSEPHINE EMPRESS OF
  FRANCE
THE KISS OF PARIS
THE KISS OF THE DEVIL
A KISS OF SILK
THE KNAVE OF
  HEARTS
THE LEAPING FLAME
A LIGHT TO THE HEART
LIGHTS OF LOVE
THE LITTLE PRETENDER
LOST ENCHANTMENT
LOST LOVE
LOVE AND LINDA
LOVE AT FORTY
LOVE FORBIDDEN
LOVE HOLDS THE
  CARDS
LOVE IN HIDING
LOVE IN PITY
LOVE IS AN EAGLE
LOVE IS CONTRABAND
LOVE IS DANGEROUS
LOVE IS MINE
LOVE IS THE ENEMY
LOVE ME FOREVER
LOVE ON THE RUN
LOVE TO THE RESCUE
LOVE UNDER FIRE
THE MAGIC OF HONEY
MESSENGER OF LOVE
METTERNICH: THE
  PASSIONATE
  DIPLOMAT
MONEY, MAGIC AND
  MARRIAGE
NO HEART IS FREE
THE ODIOUS DUKE
OPEN WINGS
OUT OF REACH

THE PASSIONATE
  PILGRIM
THE PRETTY
  HORSEBREAKERS
THE PRICE IS LOVE
A RAINBOW TO HEAVEN
THE RELUCTANT BRIDE
THE RUNAWAY HEART
THE SCANDALOUS LIFE
  OF KING CAROL
THE SECRET FEAR
THE SMUGGLED HEART
A SONG OF LOVE
STARS IN MY HEART
STOLEN HALO
SWEET ADVENTURE
SWEET ENCHANTRESS
SWEET PUNISHMENT
THEFT OF A HEART
THE THIEF OF LOVE
THIS TIME IT'S LOVE
TOUCH A STAR
TOWARDS THE STARS
THE UNKNOWN HEART
THE UNPREDICTABLE
  BRIDE
A VIRGIN IN PARIS
WE DANCED ALL NIGHT
WHERE IS LOVE?
THE WINGS OF ECSTASY
THE WINGS OF LOVE
WINGS ON MY HEART
WOMAN—THE ENIGMA

CAMFIELD
NOVELS OF LOVE

THE POOR GOVERNESS
WINGED VICTORY
LUCKY IN LOVE
LOVE AND THE MARQUIS
A MIRACLE IN MUSIC
LIGHT OF THE GODS
BRIDE TO A BRIGAND
LOVE COMES WEST

A NEW CAMFIELD NOVEL OF LOVE BY

BARBARA CARTLAND

Bride to a Brigand

A JOVE BOOK

BRIDE TO A BRIGAND

A Jove Book/published by arrangement with
the author

PRINTING HISTORY
Jove edition/April 1984

ISBN: 0-515-07308-3

Jove books are published by The Berkley Publishing Group,
200 Madison Avenue, New York, N.Y. 10016.
The words "A JOVE BOOK" and the "J" with sunburst
are trademarks belonging to Jove Publications, Inc.

PRINTED IN THE UNITED STATES OF AMERICA

Author's Note

THE Pallikares were a legendary tribe of mercenaries, brigands and robbers from the Albanian mountains. They fought magnificently in the Greek War of Independence and when it was over, the young, handsome King Otho appointed their Chief—General Xristodòlous Hadjy-Petros as his *Aide-de-Camp*.

The Albanian Chief became the most talked-of man at Court and the women fawned upon him. He was very tall, handsome, ferocious-looking and seductive, despite the fact that he was over sixty.

He wore the Albanian costume of crimson and gold embroideries and he and his followers bristled with pistols and daggers which they never hesitated to use.

The General's horses were bridled and saddled in gold and silver and his men swaggered about, wildly moustachioed and reeking of garlic. They wore great shaggy fur cloaks which made some people think they looked like the mountain bears. But others compared them to wasps, owing to their unusual habit of tight-lacing to give themselves incredibly small waists.

Ruthless, theatrical and romantic, the ladies of Athens lost their hearts, and even the Queen had a tender regard for the General.

One of the spectacular tricks of the Pallikares was to shoot a pheasant at full gallop. Other tricks were more formidable, like swooping down from the mountains and snatching up a prize horse or a pretty woman and vanishing, leaving the owner with no idea of what had happened to them.

It was a life of hardship, adventure and exploration.

chapter one

1850

"No! No! No!"

Princess Ileana's voice rang out in the high-ceilinged room and seemed to echo back at her.

Standing beside her Crown Prince Tomilav said:

"You have to marry somebody, Ileana, and I cannot think why it should not be me!"

He spoke in a somewhat sour voice because he was a handsome young man and accustomed to being adulated by the women in his own country.

As a Royal Prince of Moldavia he was well aware of his own consequence, and he found it infuriating and at the same time humiliating that the woman he loved should refuse every proposal of marriage he had made to her.

"I have no intention of marrying anybody!" Princess Ileana said in reply to his last remark.

Prince Tomilav stared at her in astonishment.

"That is a ridiculous statement," he said. "Of course you have to be married!"

"Why?"

"Do I really have to put it bluntly? Your father is dying and Zokāla must have a King."

"I intend to be Queen, and I shall rule far better than some foreigner could, who does not understand our people."

"If you are referring to me," Prince Tomilav said angrily, "that is a most unfair comment. Your people and mine are not unalike, although I admit yours are a strange mixture."

Princess Ileana smiled, and it made her look very beautiful.

"Hungarians, Rumanians, Serbians," she said softly, "all mixed together in a bowl which is Zokāla and the result is, you must admit, very attractive."

"You are speaking of yourself," Prince Tomilav said, "and you are the most beautiful person I have ever seen! Marry me, Ileana, and I swear I will make you very happy!"

Ileana looked at him and her strange green eyes had for the moment a softer expression in them as she said:

"Dear Tomilav, we have known each other since we were children, and I know that, while you are a charming man, I should after two or three days of marriage, feel like murdering you!"

"But why?" Prince Tomilav asked sharply.

"Because you would bore me," Ileana said. "All men bore me when I know them well. Only horses are never disappointing!"

She walked away from him as she spoke to look out over the valley which lay beneath the Palace.

Zokāla was a small country consisting entirely of mountains, rivers and a few valleys which were fertile enough to supply its inhabitants with most of the food they required.

Bordered by the three much larger countries Ileana had just mentioned, it had a unique position, and the throne which was just about to become empty since the King was dying seemed exceedingly desirable to all the younger Princes in the Balkans.

But it was not only the country that attracted them but the beauty of King Milko's only daughter who had all the qualities that the men of the Balkans found desirable and irresistible.

To begin with, she was a magnificent horsewoman; an Amazon whom nobody could beat in wild gallops over the Steppes.

She looked superb and she had designed for herself remarkable riding-clothes which made her look even more alluring.

To the horror and consternation of the older generation she usually rode astride, wearing a dashing coat of blue and scarlet, belted and barred like a Cossack's uniform with silver cartridge holders.

Top-boots and a fur cap of either white fox or sable completed her appearance.

She was utterly fearless, choosing always the most challenging stallions of which even her grooms were afraid.

She would outride the *Aides-de-Camp* who escorted her, and often the troops of Cavalry streaming after her across-country could not keep up.

It was strange that King Milko who was a handsome but conservative man and a stickler for tradition, should have produced a child who defied every social regulation, and whose temperament in one small person appeared to challenge the world.

Her mother, who had died when Ileana was quite

young, had been a great beauty, her blood a mixture of Russian and Hungarian, which perhaps accounted for some of the wild streak in her daughter.

Those who knew Ileana well found her unique, and knew there was nobody like her either in looks or in character.

When her father fell ill and the doctors shook their heads, and said there was no chance of saving him, Ileana through sheer force of personality had taken into her hands the reins of Government.

The Statesmen who expected easily to overrule a woman, whatever her rank, found themselves having to accept her judgements without being able to challenge them.

It was the Prime Minister and the Cabinet who more than anyone else wanted Ileana to marry, so that they might have not a woman to deal with whom they found devious and unpredictable, but a man who they felt would be far more amenable.

The Prime Minister had in fact, made it very clear to the neighbouring countries what was required.

The Princes had needed little encouragement to come pouring in from Boznia, Albania, Rumania, Montenegro and Greece.

To a younger son, who had no chance of succeeding to his father's throne, it was a Heaven-sent opportunity to reign over one of the most attractive countries in the whole of the Balkans in addition to marrying its most beautiful woman.

Ileana however had other ideas.

She refused them, laughed at them, and sent them

away saying she wished to sit on the throne alone.

This was received as being quite impossible, and those of the Princes who were not insulted by such a cavalier attitude returned to try and try again.

Prince Tomilav was very persistent.

In fact, as he said now, he was genuinely in love.

"Why will you not listen to me, Ileana," he asked, "and understand that, whatever you may say, we are eminently suited to each other?"

"That is what you may think!"

"But, I love you! You know I love you as a woman, and if you were a peasant I should still want you."

"If I were a peasant," Ileana replied scornfully, "you would ask me to occupy a very different place in your life!"

"But I would still love you, I would still make you very happy!"

There was a note of passion in Prince Tomilav's voice which she did not miss, and instinctively she moved a little way away from him.

"I do not want love!"

"You do not want love?" the Prince repeated. "What do you mean by that?"

"I mean exactly what I say. Love is a maudlin emotion exaggerated and ridiculously eulogised by poets."

"You do not know what you are talking about!"

"Fortunately I do!" Ileana said. "I have listened to you and a dozen other men telling me how I affect their hearts and how once I am in their arms they will make me feel as they do, knowing all the time it is untrue!"

"You know nothing of love because you are so young," the Prince said a little uncertainly.

Ileana laughed.

"That is what you tell yourself. I have never been in love because neither you, nor any of the other men I have ever met, has had the power to make me feel anything except that they are exceedingly boring when they become rapturous over sensations that I shall never feel."

"How do you know you will never feel them?"

"Because I am differently made, if you like, from other women."

She paused to think before she went on:

"What thrills me is knowing that the horse I am schooling has to obey me, that fight though he may, I shall always be his master. Nothing a man could give me could equal the excitement of riding at full gallop on an animal that is faster than any of the others which I follow."

The Prince drew in his breath.

It was not what Ileana said, but the sensuous excitement in her voice which roused him and made him know that he would give everything he possessed to make her feel the same way about him.

Instinctively he moved nearer and put out his arms towards her.

Without turning her head and still looking out onto the valley Ileana said:

"If you touch me, Tomilav, I will never speak to you again!"

6

For a moment he hesitated. Then he dropped his arms to his sides.

"Damn you, Ileana!" he said after a moment. "You drive a man mad!"

"So you have told me dozens of times before! Now for goodness sake, go away, because I have the Prime Minister waiting for me, and I should not be wasting time listening to you."

"Do you really think it is a waste of time?"

The hurt in the Prince's voice seemed to strike a chord in Ileana which made her say more gently:

"You know at times, I like being with you, Tomilav, and I admit you are an excellent horseman. But you merely become insufferable when you drool on about love, which is something that does not interest me."

She saw the Prince's lips tighten and added:

"We will meet at dinner tonight, and I have arranged that we shall dance afterwards, even though it will doubtless scandalise the old gossips because Papa is so ill."

"They can hardly expect you to sit crying every night at his bedside when he has been in a coma for nearly five months!" Tomilav said as if he must speak up in her defence.

"I agree with you," Ileana replied. "Therefore, although it is a small party, we shall dance, and I have asked the Gypsies to play for us."

The Prince stared at her.

"Is that wise?"

"What do you mean—is that wise?"

7

"You know that mixing with the Gypsies is not considered correct. No-one should invite them into a private home, and especially not the Palace!"

Ileana laughed and again her voice seemed to echo round the high room with its painted ceiling.

"That is what you may think in Moldavia," she said, "but here the Gypsies are a part of us, and of our lives."

Because he knew it was pointless to say any more, Tomilav shrugged his shoulders.

He thought that Ileana was inviting unnecessary criticism, and already not only the citizens of her own country, but the whole of the Balkans talked of her escapades with bated breath.

It was not only that she rode astride and that she raced against the young noblemen of Zokāla. She also competed with jockeys and professional horse-breakers and beat them too.

Dressed like a man, she had been known to climb to the top of the highest mountains in Zokāla.

In the summer, defying every convention that concerned women, she would swim in the lakes which lay under the towering peaks and even in the hottest days of summer were as cold as the glaciers above them.

There were not in fact, likely to be many spectators about in that isolated part of the country, but it was known that she behaved outrageously by swimming in a tightly-fitting costume which revealed the curves of her figure.

Stories about Ileana had been multiplying ever since

at fifteen her beauty had stunned everybody who saw her.

Many of the tales told about her were true, many untrue, but as her personality developed over the years, it was impossible to ignore her.

Travellers moving from one Balkan country to another found almost the first question they were asked as they set foot over the border was:

"What is the Princess Ileana of Zokāla doing now?"

What she was actually doing was enjoying herself.

As soon as her father became too ill to interfere with her or show his authority in any way, she had dismissed any Lady-in-Waiting who found fault with her.

She changed the *Aides-de-Camp* for younger men who made no effort to curb her exploits, and she did exactly what she pleased, besides making it quite clear who governed the country, as her father was unable to do.

Now having said goodbye to Prince Tomilav and leaving him disconsolate though still determined to go on trying to make her marry him, Ileana walked along the corridor which led to the Council Chamber.

With the sun coming through the windows to illumine her hair, bringing out the touches of vivid red which were inherited from her Hungarian ancestors, she looked like a young Diana, Goddess of the Chase.

It was a very apt description because she was thinking that as soon as she could rid herself of the Statesmen who had requested an audience she would ride down into the valley.

She would order two of her *Aides-de-Camp* to accompany her so that she could race her latest acquisition, a black stallion she had named *Satan,* against them.

Satan was justly named because he was ferocious, with what the grooms described as a fiendish temper, and he had already injured three stable-boys who attempted to saddle him.

To Ileana he was a challenge and a delight, and if she dreamed of anybody in her huge blue velvet bed with its carved headboard and canopy supported by golden angels, it was of *Satan*.

The Palace of Zokāla was one of the most romantic in the whole world.

Ileana's grandmother, having fallen passionately in love with her husband after a marriage which had been arranged simply because it was politically suitable, had determined to create a background to match the romantic fervour of her heart.

She had therefore called in the finest Zokālan craftsmen who were traditionally very clever carvers, painters and decorators, to tell them what she required.

As they had previously been ignored by the Royal Family it was a delight for them to create a fairy-tale Palace of such beauty and with such imagination that everybody who saw it gasped in wonder.

It had been a fitting background for Ileana's mother also who had been very beautiful, and now for Ileana herself.

Those who saw her against the malachite and pink marble pillars, the painted ceilings, the gold and silver walls, the exquisite beauty of domes and spires, the courtyards embellished with brilliant mosaics, thought they must have stepped into a fairy-story.

Because Ileana was so lovely, her gown which had been designed and made for her in Paris, made her look like a painting by Winterhalter.

And if there had been cupids carrying garlands of roses flying ahead of her nobody would have been surprised.

At the same time, as she entered the Council Chamber her green eyes were shrewd and wary, because her intuition told her that what she was going to hear from the Statesmen who had demanded her audience would be far from pleasant.

She was however surprised when she entered the great room with a polished table down the centre of it at which thirty people could sit in comfort.

She had expected there to be at least a dozen men waiting for her, but instead there was only the Prime Minister and the Lord Chamberlain.

The Prime Minister was shorter than most Zokālans, who were a tall race, and perhaps because of his Office he had a permanently worried expression.

He was, as Ileana knew, an extremely clever man and had the future prosperity of the country very much at heart.

The Lord Chamberlain, who was growing old, was a staunch Royalist, and Ileana knew she could rely on him to support her on any problem which concerned the prestige of the Monarchy.

She walked towards them as they bowed their heads,

and having greeted them with a smile she seated herself in the high-backed carved chair which at the head of the table looked not unlike a throne.

It had, of course, been designed for a man.

She therefore looked somewhat insubstantial against the Zokālan coat-of-arms emblazoned at the back of it surmounted by a gilded crown.

"I am delighted to see you, Prime Minister," she said, "but I am surprised that you are not accompanied by more of your colleagues."

"We felt, Your Royal Highness, that what we have to say should be discussed by as few people as possible until you have made a decision."

Ileana looked from one man to the other, then gave a little sigh.

She was quite certain that what she was about to hear was something she had heard a dozen times already.

"What is it?" she enquired.

"The Lord Chamberlain and I have come to ask Your Royal Highness if you will make a decision as soon as possible as to who will be our future King."

"I thought perhaps that was what was in your mind," Ileana replied, "but you know as well as I do, Prime Minister, that I have no intention of marrying anybody!"

"That is what Your Royal Highness has said before," the Prime Minister said quietly, "but now circumstances make it imperative that you should be married, and as quickly as possible!"

There was a note in his voice which made Ileana

look at him searchingly before she asked:

"What has happened that you have not told me? Why is there this sudden urgency that has not, apparently, been brought to the attention of the whole Council?"

The Prime Minister glanced across the table at the Lord Chamberlain as if for support before he said:

"We have just learnt, Your Royal Highness, that an armed tribe led by General Vladilas is camping in the mountains on the other side of the valley."

Ileana looked puzzled.

"General Vladilas?" she enquired. "I do not seem to have heard of him before."

"He leads a nomadic tribe of brigands and robbers who have been talked about for some years now, in all neighbouring countries, but they have only just become a problem to us."

Ileana was interested.

"Tell me about them."

As she spoke she put her elbows on the table and rested her chin in her hands, thinking that this was certainly something she had not expected.

She was aware that almost as if he was afraid he might frighten her the Prime Minister was choosing his words before he said:

"I presume Your Royal Highness has heard of the Pallikares?"

"Of course, I have heard of them," Ileana replied, "but I do not know a great deal about them."

"The main body of the tribe has always been situated in Greece..."

"Oh, now I know who you are talking about!" Ileana interrupted. "They are legendary, and I believe magnificent fighting men."

"That is true," the Prime Minister agreed, "but while they might be serviceable to a country in wartime, they can be a menace in time of peace!"

As he was talking Ileana thought back to what she had heard of the Pallikares.

Somebody had described them to her once as the most picturesque men in Northern Greece.

"Their costumes are all gold-embroidered," her informant had said, "they bristle with pistols and *Yataghans* which they do not hesitate to use, and their horses are trapped out in silver and gold."

"They sound entrancing!" Ileana had remarked.

"Actually the men swagger about wildly moustachioed, wearing shaggy fur coats and look like great bears."

What she had been told about them had captured Ileana's imagination, but it had been a long time ago.

Now she remembered clearly what had been said, and how she had always hoped one day to see the Pallikares but had thought it unlikely.

"Why have they come here?" she asked.

The Prime Minister made a gesture with his hands.

"I cannot give Your Royal Highness an answer to that question," he said. "The Lord Chamberlain and I have been discussing it on our way here and my opinion is that they mean trouble."

"What sort of trouble?"

"If there are a large number of them they could

practically take over part of the country."

"Do you mean go to war with us?"

The Prime Minister drew in his breath.

"I am afraid, Your Royal Highness, that the answer to that is 'Yes,' but in a different manner from the way we understand war. They are men of the mountains who come down to the plains, seize what they want whether it is food, possessions or women, and disappear back to where they came from before anything can be done about it."

"And to prevent this from happening you think that we should expel them by force?"

There was a pause before the Prime Minister replied:

"I believe that our Army, small though it is, could defeat and drive away the Pallikares."

His eyes met Ileana's as he spoke, and she faced him defiantly.

"What you are saying, Prime Minister, is that you require me to marry so that I can give you a man at the head of our troops whom the whole country will follow."

"Your Royal Highness has put the words into my mouth!" the Prime Minister said with a note of satisfaction in his voice.

"Then you really think," Ileana said after a moment, "that our Generals are not capable of fighting these vagabonds on their own?"

The Prime Minister looked worried.

"Believe me, Your Royal Highness, we do not yet know the numbers of the tribe, but they are certain to be considerable. General Vladilas is known and feared in Bulgaria, and there are rumours of his exploits in Albania."

"How old is he?"

"I have no idea, Your Royal Highness. In fact, he is something of a mystery man. People talk about him, and the legends of his invincibility have grown until the mere fact that he is challenging us, if that is what he means to do, will frighten our people, unless they are assured that we have somebody of his stature to face him."

"A King!" Ileana said almost beneath her breath.

"Exactly!" the Prime Minister agreed. "We need a young King who will lead our troops and whom they will follow because they both admire and respect him."

It was then that the Lord Chamberlain, who had been silent up until now, spoke for the first time.

"It is not only arms, Your Royal Highness, which win battles," he said, "it is the spirit of the fighting men who use them, and behind the fighting men is the spirit of the people they defend."

"I understand what you are saying, My Lord Chamberlain," Ileana replied, "but where are we to find such a man?"

There was silence, and she knew that the Prime Minister was thinking over the list of her numerous suitors and wondering which of them would best fill the place waiting for him.

Before he could speak she asked:

"Do you really believe that a foreigner, however Royal his blood may be, could not only represent Zo-kāla at a moment's notice, but capture the imagination of the people and win their confidence in the way you describe?"

She spoke scornfully, then before either of the Statesmen could answer her she said:

"His only asset would be that he was married to me. I will lead my own troops in my own way, and make sure that if these cutthroats try to injure Zokāla, we will drive them away in a manner which will ensure that they never attack us again!"

Now the Prime Minister and the Lord Chamberlain turned to stare at her in sheer astonishment.

The Prime Minister was the first to find his voice.

"What you are suggesting is impossible, Your Royal Highness, absolutely impossible!"

"Why?"

"Quite simply because you are a woman!"

"Then you do not agree that I have far more determination and a far greater grasp of what is required, as well as far more love for my country, than any outsider could possibly have?"

"Of course! Of course!" the Prime Minister agreed. "That is obvious! But no country could possibly be led into battle by a woman!"

"There were women in history who did exactly that!"

"That was many hundreds of years ago," the Prime Minister said, "but not today, not with modern weapons."

"Do you really think it matters particularly," Ileana asked, "whether one is killed by an arrow or a piece of lead? If one is going to die, one dies."

"This conversation is merely speculative, Your Royal

Highness," the Lord Chamberlain interrupted, "and we are very serious. We can only beg you now not to dismiss our petition as a jest or something of little importance."

"I am not doing that," Ileana murmured.

"What we are asking," the Lord Chamberlain went on as if she had not spoken, "is that Your Royal Highness should accept one of the many suitors for your hand who have been travelling in and out of the country during the last six months, raising our hopes only to have them dashed as they departed."

The way he spoke made Ileana know that it would be a mistake to tease him or to argue any further.

Instead in the calm, businesslike manner in which she usually addressed the Council Meetings she said:

"I appreciate that you have brought this problem to me before it has been discussed openly with your colleagues. I would like a little time to think it over, and as soon as I have come to a decision I will inform you of it."

She saw the expression of relief on both men's faces before the Prime Minister said:

"That is very gratifying, Your Royal Highness, and we can only thank you for understanding that the position is extremely precarious, and we do not wish to frighten our people unless it is absolutely necessary."

"No, no, of course not!" Ileana agreed. "But I would like a report from the Generals on what troops we have at our disposal, and I would also like to know, as early as possible, the numbers and, of course, the intentions of the Pallikares."

There was a little silence before the Prime Minister said:

"I regret, Your Royal Highness, that we find our espionage in this particular has not proved as effective as we might have hoped."

"What do you mean—not effective?" Ileana asked sharply. "I had always understood that the branch of the Army which specialises in Intelligence was considered extremely efficient!"

The Prime Minister looked embarrassed and Ileana asked:

"What has happened?"

"It is extremely regrettable," the Prime Minister replied, "that after Colonel Bartik died, nobody was appointed in his place."

Ileana looked at the Prime Minister in astonishment.

"Do you mean to tell me that we have no Army Intelligence operating at this moment?"

"Shall we say it has not been properly co-ordinated since the Colonel's death," the Prime Minister answered, and she was aware that he was nervous.

"It is extremely remiss, and most unfortunate at this particular moment!" Ileana said sharply. "I blame myself that I had not thought of it before."

"It was certainly not your duty to do so," the Lord Chamberlain remarked, "but as Your Royal Highness is well aware, the older Generals dislike anything that seems to them modern in the way of training, and prefer keeping to the traditional methods of warfare, which except in Russia do not include espionage."

"But why not at this moment, when we need spies?

Spies who will infiltrate the Pallikares tribe, spies to tell us what their intentions are, and spies to discover whether General Vladilas is as menacing as you seem to think?"

"I can only agree with Your Royal Highness," the Prime Minister said sheepishly, "but without Colonel Bartik we had no idea how to set about doing such things."

Ileana tapped her fingers on the table.

"There must be many adventurous young men in the Army who would welcome the assignment of finding out what we want to know."

"I am afraid such matters are beyond my comprehension," the Prime Minister said. "I imagine if the Pallikares under General Vladilas are in the mountains where we are told they are camping, they will have a 'bird's eye view' over the valley."

"I have to admit that is a reasonable supposition," Ileana replied.

She was thinking as she spoke of the magnificent view she had been afforded over the whole valley when she had climbed to the top of Mount Bela and had seen the Palace below her looking like a child's doll's house.

It would be impossible for any soldier to approach such a position without the Pallikares seeing him and if they wished shooting him down.

It suddenly seemed to Ileana to be a far more complex problem than she had at first thought.

At the same time she told herself that if she could

not find a solution it was unlikely that a foreign husband, if she had one, would do any better.

She was however, well aware that what the Prime Minister and the Lord Chamberlain were demanding of her was reasonable in the circumstances.

Ileana knew that Zokālan women, like the women in most of the other Balkan countries, kept their place, which was behind the man, not even beside him.

They might rule their homes, and undoubtedly the more spirited of them did.

But they played no part in business, in politics, in any affairs concerning the nation as a whole.

In one district Bulgarian women even waited on their husbands and were not allowed to sit at the table with them, while the average Zokālan man believed that women were meant for pleasure and for very little else.

Because she was more perturbed by what she had heard than she liked to admit, Ileana rose to her feet.

"As I have already said, Gentlemen," she said, "I will think over the problem and let you have an answer as quickly as possible, but I hope you will not press me too hard."

She smiled, but the Prime Minister's face was serious as he replied:

"While we are deeply grateful to Your Royal Highness, we would like to point out that time is of great importance. The Pallikares might make up their minds to strike as early as tomorrow or the next day. We do not know, but we must be ready for them."

"I agree with you," Ileana answered. "At the same time, we have an old saying which tells us that it is 'wise to make haste slowly!'"

She knew as she spoke that she was being hypocritical, which was something she had never been in the past.

She had always wanted to jump every fence, sweep away every obstacle, and gain her objective the moment she had thought of it.

But she knew if she had a husband it would be something very different.

While the Prime Minister and the Lord Chamberlain bowed her out of the room with smiles of satisfaction on their lips, Ileana was telling herself she could not and would not marry in such circumstances.

This was the first time since she had grown up that she felt as if she was trapped, that iron bars were waiting to imprison her in an intolerable situation from which she shrank with every nerve in her body.

She had been quite young when she first decided that marriage was something she did not wish for herself.

She had known that her father and mother had been very happy together, but all round her were innumerable examples of men and women who were joined by what was said to be the Blessing of God, but who in fact were actively unhappy.

She had first become aware of what a woman could suffer, when she found one of her mother's Ladies-in-Waiting, the Baroness Spryidon, weeping bitterly in the garden where she had not expected to be discovered.

Ileana supposed she must have injured herself, and she ran towards her saying:

"What has happened? Did you fall down? Can I help you?"

The Baroness, who was an extremely pretty woman and one whom Ileana had always admired, raised her face from her hands.

She saw the tears running down her cheeks and her dark eyes swimming with them.

"What is wrong?" she asked again. "Oh, please, do not cry like that."

The Baroness had drawn out a small handkerchief with which to dab her eyes.

"It is nothing, Your Royal Highness," she had replied, "and please, do not tell anybody what you have seen."

She rose from the stone seat on which she was sitting as she spoke and walked away, leaving Ileana staring after her in surprise.

She had gone back into the Palace to find her old Nurse who looked after her now that she was older in the role of a lady's-maid.

Without giving away any secrets she asked:

"I do not think the Baroness looks at all happy, Nanny, and she is very pale. Do you think she is ill?"

The old Nurse, who was an inveterate gossip, gave a little snort of indignation before she replied:

"It's her heart what's ill, an' there's no cure for that!"

"Her heart?" Ileana had asked in some surprise.

"That man ought to be ashamed of himself, that he ought!" Nanny declared. "Your father should have a sharp word with him. But there, His Majesty never sees what's going on under his very nose!"

Ileana knew that the Baron was one of her father's trusted Lords-in-Waiting.

He was a very handsome man and she had once heard somebody saying that he had a 'roving eye.'

Now suddenly she understood what it meant.

That night before going to bed, she had seen the Baron in close conversation with another Lady-in-Waiting who had only recently taken up her duties and was young and attractive.

She was married, but her husband was serving with the Army, and she had for the first week or two seemed to be somewhat at a loose end, Ileana had thought.

Now as she watched them, it was very obvious that the Baron's advances were welcome and she responded with sparkling eyes and smiling lips.

"How can he be so unkind to his wife as to make her cry?" Ileana asked.

Then for the first time she began to look around the Court and found that it was very different from what it had seemed to her when a child.

Then everybody had appeared to be happy, laughing, enjoying life as she did, and she had always believed every couple was as content with each other as her father and mother were.

Now it was as if an evil fairy pointed out the flaws in everything that before had seemed perfect and un-blemished.

She discovered that the Baron paid attention to every new face, leaving a trail of broken hearts behind him.

The Baroness grew paler, thinner, and sadder, and although Ileana never found her crying again, she was certain it was something she did in the privacy of her own room.

She felt even more angry and resentful when she learnt that an irate husband had challenged the Baron to a duel which had been fought in the Palace grounds at dawn.

Unfortunately and unfairly it was the husband who had been wounded, while the Baron bounced back, gyrating as usual in the direction of the latest pretty face to arrive in the Palace.

He certainly had a wide choice because the Zokālan ladies were exceptionally lovely.

It was then, quite by chance while out riding, Ileana saw the Baron behaving outrageously with a very young, very beautiful peasant-girl, and now under-standing what he was really like, she convinced herself that all other men were the same.

From that moment she decided that she would never allow herself to be so humiliated.

No man should treat her as if she was a flower to be plucked and enjoyed for a short time, only to be thrown aside when the scent no longer attracted him.

Almost as if the rose-coloured spectacles through which she had seen the world as a child had been whisked away from her eyes, everywhere she looked she found men being unfaithful to their wives.

Then the women they had finished with were thrown aside to cry miserably and presumably were expected to be content with their memories.

"That will never happen to me!" Ileana vowed.

Yet now, at this moment, she was confronted with a problem she could not ignore, or push aside.

She had taken it upon herself since her father's illness to rule Zokāla.

How could she refuse to give the country she loved and which she thought of as belonging to her, the leader it required, and who traditionally must be a man?

chapter two

ILEANA looked round the table in the Council Chamber and decided that the Senior Officers of the Army were all too old.

They looked magnificent in their uniforms glistening with medals and gold braid, but many of them had bald heads, a number wore spectacles, and there was almost no officer who had not begun to show grey hairs on his temples.

She had called an Army Conference first thing in the morning, and she knew as they stood and bowed when she joined them that they were apprehensive about what she had to say.

Because she wished them to forget that she was a woman she was wearing her riding-clothes.

She was aware they averted their gaze from her legs which showed beneath the tailored coat with its Cossacklike silver cartridge holders and the severe leather belt which encircled her small waist.

But however masculine her clothes were, she could not disguise the very feminine beauty of her red gold hair; her large, dark-fringed green eyes, or the translucent quality of her skin.

Her voice however was strictly formal as she said:

"Good-morning, Gentlemen! I have called you here having received grave news from the Prime Minister."

She knew that they thought she was referring to the proximity of the Pallikares, but when she went on the expressions on their faces changed.

"I am astonished, in fact astounded," she said, "to learn that Colonel Bartik's place, after he died, has not been filled!"

She looked severely at the General sitting next to her and asked:

"Can you explain this omission, General?"

There was a perceptible pause before the General replied:

"We considered, Your Royal Highness, that our Army was efficient without the need for the type of service supplied to us by the Colonel."

"And now you have been proved wrong," Ileana said sharply, "for nobody appears to have any idea how many of the Pallikares, if that is who they are, are camping in the mountains and whether they come in peace, or with the intention of causing trouble."

Her voice was sharp and she was aware the Generals sitting next to her shifted uncomfortably in their seats.

"I can only condemn in no uncertain language," she went on, "this omission, and ask you to inform me what you intend to do about it."

The Officers sitting round the table now looked even more uncomfortable than they had before.

They glanced at each other surreptitiously and she was aware the problem had not been raised until this moment, and they had no answer.

After a very uncomfortable silence Ileana asked:

"How many of the men in our Armed Forces are experienced mountain climbers?"

Again there was silence until one officer said tentatively:

"We have always relied, Your Royal Highness, on the men whose sole occupation it is to climb the mountains, either for pleasure or because they have constituted themselves a rescue team, to help anybody who is in trouble."

"That appears to me to be a very slipshod way of conducting the defence of our country!"

As if at last she had aroused them into making some report a Senior General, a man of over sixty said pompously:

"I am quite certain, Your Royal Highness, that if the Pallikares are here and do intend to attack us, our Army will not fail to distinguish itself and drive them away."

"That is all very well, General," Ileana retorted, "but you speak as if you expected them to be drawn up in front of you on the plain, advancing in the old-fashioned manner with swords or spears in their hands!"

She looked round the table with a contemptuous expression in her eyes as she continued:

"I am interested to know what you would do if they opened fire on us from the mountain heights where you cannot reach them: and then if while you are withdrawing ineffectually, they swooped down to pillage our crops, our herds and anything else on which they can lay their hands."

Again there was a pregnant silence until Ileana said sharply:

"I wish to receive promptly a report on what defence you intend to put up against the Pallikares, and also any other information you can obtain about them."

She paused to add bitterly:

"I can only say that if my father were well enough to understand what is happening, he would be appalled at the complacency and lack of initiative in the Zokālan Army of which he has always been so proud."

With that she rose from the table and walked away in silence, leaving the Officers standing and staring after her with a grave look on their faces.

Outside she told herself she might have routed them, but it would not be so easy to do the same to General Vladilas, if he had superior weapons that were more modern than those they possessed.

In that case he could, if that was what he intended, take over the whole country.

"How can it possibly have come to this?" she asked herself angrily.

She knew that even before her father had sunk into his present coma he had been content to let things drift, to believe what old men like himself both in the Army and Parliament told him.

And worst of all, to be positively against any change in the *status quo*.

Now as she reached the Library where she usually sat when she was dealing with Affairs of State, she wondered frantically what she should do, and how she could with a wave of a magic wand transform an ancient and creaking machine at a moment's notice into a modern, efficient one.

"It is impossible!" she admitted.

At the same time, she told herself that the Prime Minister's idea of her quickly finding a husband to lead them was about as useless as the guns they used would be against men who were camped high in the mountains where the shells would never reach them.

Too restless and worried to sit down, she walked up and down the room, striving to find some solution.

She knew as she did so that if she failed, if the Pallikares took over the country, or even merely raided and devastated it, the outside world would blame her.

"The woman should have married long ago!" the neighbouring Crowned Heads would say. "Her husband could have introduced new ideas, modern methods, and certainly new weapons!"

It was an argument which would end with their saying scornfully:

"Women know nothing of Armies, of strategy and tactics, and why should they?"

"How could I have been so blind, so stupid as to not have thought of this before?" Ileana asked herself.

For the first time she realised she had spent too much time with the Cavalry Officers because they rode so well and shared her love of horses.

She had forgotten that guns and rifles were what an enemy would use in modern warfare.

Two months ago she had attended the manoeuvres

which took place every year, and in her father's absence had taken the salute as the Regiments of soldiers marched on the level ground below the Palace.

It had all been very impressive, and the music of the Bands, the waving pennants carried by the Cavalry, the ceremony of trooping the Regimental Colours, were very moving.

Now she felt it had all been a sham. She should not only have admired the horses and the men who rode them, but should have demanded to know what other weapons the Zokālan Army had at its disposal.

She had the uncomfortable feeling that the guns, each drawn into the Parade Ground by six magnificent horses, were out of date and capable of little more than firing a Royal Salute.

She also remembered there had been remarkably few of them and wondered how her father could have omitted to ask for a detailed account of expenditure on defence during the last few years.

He should have made sure that the money allowed to the Army was spent not only on horses and uniforms, but on weapons.

What was worse was the loss of Colonel Bartik. She had the feeling that he had always been treated as something of a joke by the older Ministers, and by her father.

"The Russians have spies everywhere," she had heard him say once, "although, Heaven knows, most countries would be only too willing to tell them what they are trying to find out without their sending ferret-faced men to look under the beds and listen at doors."

There was of course, a roar of laughter round the dining-table, and he went on:

"The only advantage of such curiosity from our point of view is that many of the Tsar's Secret Agents are very beautiful women, and it is a pleasure to whisper secrets into their shell-like ears!"

His remark had caused a great deal of laughter and one General whom Ileana had always thought of as a 'stick-in-the-mud' remarked:

"Personally, I have no secrets, and I doubt if the most astute and beautiful Russian could find anything worth investigating in Zokāla!"

This statement had been received with applause, and Ileana now thought they had been living in a 'Fool's Paradise.'

The smaller Balkan States had always been in fear of their larger neighbours.

Dobruja had been shuffled backwards and forwards between Rumania and Russia, and there had been beady eyes on Montenegro both from Boznia and from Serbia.

"How could we have been so blind as not to realise that Zokāla would be a feather in the cap of Hungary or Rumania?" Ileana asked herself.

She longed to talk over what she was thinking with somebody who would understand the dangers which were only just beginning to present themselves to her mind.

But who was there?

The Generals had not been prepared to admit that they were at fault, and the politicians were, none of them, fighting men.

"There must be somebody I can consult!" Ileana told herself.

She shied away from the thought that the Prime Minister would undoubtedly tell her that it should be her husband.

But even if she consented to do as they wished and marry, who could understand their problems better than she could herself?

Certainly not Tomilav who had never served in his own Army, except as Honorary Colonel-in-Chief of some Regiment that was not already represented by his two older brothers.

Then there was Prince Georg, another suitor who came from Macedonia, but was far more knowledgeable about painting and mosaics and ancient history than anything to do with war.

The same applied, she thought, to various of her other suitors with the exception of one, Prince Ivan. But he was a Russian and merely wanted to take her away to live on his vast estates where he ruled with far more opulence and authority than any King.

"I shall have to do something about this myself," Ileana decided.

The question was—what?

Then she had an idea.

The only people who might know something about the Pallikares, if that was who they were, would be the climbers, who the General had just said the Army relied on for information concerning the mountains.

Ileana knew most of them well, for they had guided her and ensured her safety when she climbed with them, although actually it was something she had not done since last year.

It was not because she did not enjoy climbing, it was that she had become so absorbed in training her horses, buying new ones, and breaking in those that were beyond the control of her grooms, that they had left her little time for any other outdoor activities.

Now, as if the idea was like a light in the darkness, she walked from the Library into the hall of the Palace and sent footmen scurrying in every direction.

One ran to the stables to order horses, another to the *Aides-de-Camp* to bring the two men who habitually escorted her on horseback running to her side.

When they reached her they saluted smartly and she said:

"Come with me, and tell anyone who is interested that we will not be back until late."

"Very good, Your Royal Highness!"

In a few minutes they were on their way, Ileana riding *Satan,* the two men on the next fastest horses in the stable, so that they could attempt to keep up with her.

She knew as she left the Palace behind that if any of the older Courtiers had seen her go they would disapprove.

They had always thought it extremely reprehensible

that she should ride with only two escorts instead of a troop of Cavalry.

What was more, they really thought that Queens and Princesses should travel wherever they wished to go in a carriage with a Lady-in-Waiting seated opposite them.

Although the sun was already warm Ileana had not bothered to change from her severe Cossacklike uniform into one of her attractive habits that were made to suit all the seasons of the year.

Instead she merely put on a fur cap, the lightest she possessed. It was made of sable and framed her face, throwing into prominence the quality of her skin and the light in her eyes.

"Where are we going, Your Royal Highness?" Captain Heviz asked when they were some way from the Palace.

"We are on a voyage of discovery," Ileana replied, reining in *Satan* a little so that the Captain could hear what she said.

Captain Pokal, who was riding on the other side of her, remarked:

"That sounds exciting!"

"I hope it will be," Ileana answered, "because we three have to find out what our Generals have lamentably failed to do, then decide what can be done about it."

"I presume Your Royal Highness is referring to the Pallikares!"

"Of course!"

"I have heard of them for some years," Captain Pokal said, "and if you ask me, there is too much fuss being made about their arrival in our country!"

"Why do you think that?" Ileana asked.

"They are nothing but a collection of Bandits," Captain Pokal replied, "and it is absolute nonsense to suppose that they wish to take over a country like ours! What they want is loot, food of which there is plenty in the mountains at this time of the year, and when they can find one, a pretty woman!"

He spoke impulsively.

Then as if he felt it was something he should not have said in front of Ileana he coughed and looked away in an embarrassed manner.

"I had heard that already," Ileana said calmly. "At the same time, it seems strange that they should be camping on Mount Bela, unless there are a great number of them."

Neither of the *Aides-de-Camp* had any idea what she was talking about and she explained:

"I have climbed Bela, and on the other side of it there is a valley that is very beautiful, but almost uninhabited except for the occasional shepherd or game-hunter."

She could see they were both listening and she went on:

"It is a beautiful valley and one to which I have often thought we should pay more attention."

As if she was talking to herself rather than to the two men she said:

"We have always extended Northwards, but the South is warmer. There is plenty of water and the only difficulty would be communication between that area and the valley in which we are riding at the moment."

"Surely there is a way?" Captain Heviz asked as if he was not certain.

"Yes, of course," Ileana replied, "the Bela Valley is reached from the route we use to enter Bulgaria."

She remembered as she spoke how she had noticed the rough roads with high cliffs rising on each side of them when she last travelled there two years ago with her father.

It had been a tiring but exciting journey, and they had been received with great pomp and ceremony despite the fact that the Monarchy in Bulgaria was extremely unstable.

They had so many troubles of their own that Ileana thought it was very unlikely that they, at any rate, would wish to concern themselves with Zokāla.

She was intelligent enough to realise that if the Pallikares created chaos in her own country, as they might easily do, then it would be easy for Austria, Rumania or Serbia to step in.

The ostensible excuse would be to help Zokālans to restore order. The next stage would be to annex them to their own country.

"That must never happen," she told herself, but was not certain how she could prevent it.

After an hour of hard riding they had reached the foot of the Bela mountain which was the nearest to the Capital.

It was quite the most spectacular in the range which provided a natural barrier from their neighbours and was a formidable protection for Zokāla.

Built amongst the grey rocks at the foot of the mountain there were, Ileana knew, a number of small cottages, inhabited by the men who climbed the heights above them, both as a living and because it was something they enjoyed.

They were strong, magnificent to look at, and so well versed in their profession that it was very rare for a climber to injure himself or to fail to rescue either a human being or an animal in distress.

Bela was however not an easy mountain.

In many places its stone was smooth without any chance of a foothold, and it rose proudly from the plain as a result of volcanic activity which had taken place many centuries before.

When Ileana had climbed it it had been with Olav's help, and it was to him that she now intended to look for information.

He was the oldest and most experienced of the climbers and respected by everybody in the country.

When they reached his small, white cottage with its pointed roof of black slates, Captain Heviz dismounted and knocked on his door.

It was opened by Olav's wife, who curtsied respectfully when she saw it was the Princess, and without waiting hurried back into the cottage shouting her husband's name.

He came out a minute later rubbing his eyes as if to remove the sleep from them.

39

Ileana guessed he had been up late the night before, perhaps rescuing a sheep who had been marooned on a ledge from which it could not descend.

Or he might have been battling with the eagles who were known to carry off baby lambs.

Olav grinned with delight when he saw Ileana and hurried to the side of her horse to say:

"It is good to see you, Gracious Princess! I have missed you this last year. I had hoped that I might once again have the privilege of helping you to climb one of the peaks from which you can see almost the whole world."

Ileana laughed.

She enjoyed Olav's flattering way of talking.

"I have been very remiss, but you must forgive me. And now I need your help."

"My help, Gracious Lady?"

Ileana gave a signal to Captain Heviz who went to *Satan*'s head.

The horse did not like his touching his bridle and tried to rear, but Ileana controlled him, then slipped to the ground.

She walked to where outside Olav's cottage there was a rough seat which he had himself made from wood cut from the forest.

She sat down and when he stood in front of her she said:

"I think you can guess what I want to know, Olav."

"About them?"

He jerked his thumb as he spoke towards the summit of the mountain and Ileana said:

"Nobody can tell me anything about them, except that they are there. I want to know who they are, and how many?"

"That is difficult to say, Gracious Lady," Olav replied, "but many, many!"

Ileana frowned.

She wondered if Olav could count, but because she had always found him truthful she thought what he said was ominous.

"What are they doing?" she enquired.

"They are camped in tents and the caves."

"Why are they there?"

Olav shrugged his shoulders.

"They shoot goats and chamois, and race their horses..."

"Horses?" Ileana interrupted. "They have horses?"

"Many, many horses, Gracious Lady."

This was something she had not expected.

She had always supposed that as most Brigands spent their time high in the mountains, it was impossible for them to have horses with them.

Now she thought she had been very obtuse.

Vaguely at the back of her mind, although she had forgotten it until now, she remembered hearing that the Pallikares notable accomplishment was to shoot a pheasant from a horse travelling at full gallop.

Of course they would have their horses with them, and she thought now that perhaps that was another reason why they had come to Zokāla.

The horses of Zokāla were famous for their appearance, their stamina, and their speed.

Naturally there were far fewer of them than there were in Hungary, but already there was a demand for foals which gratified the horse-breeders, and a Zokálan-bred horse was looked upon with respect in all the surrounding countries.

As if he was following her thoughts Olav said:

"They very fine horsemen. I see horses race in the Bela Valley. Very Fast! Gracious Lady would enjoy it!"

Ileana drew in her breath.

She had a sudden idea that was more outrageous than any idea she had ever had before.

She looked up at the mountain towering above her.

It was formidable. At the same time, it looked very quiet and peaceful.

There were two eagles hovering overhead, and that meant, she was sure, that if any of the Pallikares were watching, their eyes would be on those.

She made up her mind.

"Take me up the mountain, Olav," she said, "just high enough for me to see what is happening on the other side."

A huge grin of delight spread over Olav's face and his eyes lit up.

"The Gracious Lady wish go now?"

"Yes, at once!" Ileana agreed.

He ran back inside the cottage to collect his ropes and all the other equipment essential to the safety of a climber.

Ileana walked slowly back to where the two *Aides-*

de-Camp were standing with the horses.

"I am going to climb up the mountain with Olav," she said.

If she had exploded a bomb at their feet they could not have looked more astonished.

"I am sure Your Royal Highness should not do such a thing!" Captain Heviz objected.

"It will be quite safe," Ileana replied. "I must find out for myself, which the Army has lamentably neglected to do, why the Pallikares have to all intents and purposes invaded us."

"But, Your Royal Highness, it may be dangerous! Suppose the Brigands capture and kill you?"

"They are not likely to do that," Ileana replied, "and since I shall not be accompanied except by Olav, they will merely think I am another tourist enjoying a quiet climb, which as you well know, happens a dozen times a day at this time of the year."

This was true.

A great number of people came to Zokāla to climb the mountains and go home to boast of their achievement.

Ileana thought she would not be surprised if the other professional climbers like Olav were not scaling the mountains further along the range which were easier than Bela and where they usually took novices.

Without listening to any more arguments from the *Aides-de-Camp* who were, in fact, too astonished to say very much, she went into the cottage where she had often been before and took off her coat.

Olav's wife rolled it into a bundle wrapped in a piece of clean muslin and gave it to her husband who carried it on his back.

It was quite common to start the day in blazing sunshine, but as they climbed higher the weather could change, and the return journey could be bitterly cold unless one had a coat to wear.

Underneath it Ileana was wearing the tight-fitting trousers which resembled those worn by the officers when they were off-duty and above them a blue silk blouse which matched her coat.

It fastened at the neck with a brooch that had been given to her on her last birthday by the Officers of the King's Cavalry which she always wore when riding with them.

Otherwise, her blouse was very plain and the only touch of colour came from the brilliant red satin sash around her waist, the ends of which fell down her hip on one side.

She looked very elegant, but she was well aware that any older members of the Court would have thought her appearance immodest and improper, and would have averted their eyes.

It was however, impossible to climb in skirts and Ileana was already an experienced climber.

Although she had not climbed with Olav for a year it was a delight to walk lithely along in the climbing shoes he always kept for her in his cottage, and into which she had changed from her riding-boots.

She felt almost as if she had wings on her feet as

they moved very quickly over the rocks and stones at the foot of the mountains.

Then they reached the hard rock that had to be climbed carefully because there were so few footholds.

For Olav it was as easy as walking upstairs and having attached his ropes to Ileana he led the way knowing that he had taught her never to make an unwary step, never to move until she was quite certain she would not slip.

The sun was high in the sky as they climbed steadily.

It took them over an hour to reach the point from which Ileana knew she could look down into the valley on the other side and see what was happening.

There was no sound except for the tap of Olav's alpine pick, and they did not speak.

She knew without her telling him that Olav was aware that this was a secret climb, that she was spying on the intruders and had no wish for them to be aware of it.

All the time they were climbing higher she could see the eagles overhead and this reassured her that whatever was happening in the Bela Valley it was unlikely that there were human beings just above them on this side of the mountains.

Olav stopped just short of the top, and turning round pulled the ropes that drew Ileana up beside him.

Then as he put out his hand to take hers she joined him, crawling forward so that she would not be seen from below silhouetted against the sky.

They were on a narrow ledge from which on one side the peak of the mountain rose straight up, while below them it sloped down into the valley, mush less steeply than on the side which they had just climbed.

By craning her neck Ileana could just see what lay below her.

Olav had been right.

There were many, many men who looked like little ants moving about, and to her surprise, pitched directly below these were a number of quite large tents of various brilliant colours.

It was not the tents however that held Ileana's attention, but the horses on the plain and there were far more of them than she had expected.

She realised as she looked that they were being drilled into pulling a number of large guns, so large that even at this distance she knew they were bigger than anything her own Army possessed.

She counted up to ten of them, then realised that those were only the ones being drawn by teams of six horses each.

On each side of the ground there were guns and more guns.

The men were sitting watching what was taking place, each of them carrying a rifle on his back and although she could not see very clearly Ileana was sure there were pistols and knives in the sash around their waists.

She drew in her breath at the horror of what she was seeing.

Then as she was about to tell Olav they should

descend because it was dangerous to remain any longer, men materialised as if out of nowhere on each side of them.

They looked just as she had expected the Pallikares would look: large, strong, bristling with weapons, and most of them, despite the heat, wearing sheepskin *shoudas* and fur caps which she knew were called *kalpaks*.

It was then her heart gave a frightened thump, but speaking calmly and slowly she said:

"Good-day to you! I have just, as you see, climbed the mountain with my friend!"

She indicated Olav with her hand, then realising that the men facing her did not understand she spoke to them instead in Bulgarian.

For a moment she thought that once again she had drawn a blank.

Then one man moved forward to answer her.

"You boy?" he asked.

As he spoke he looked at Ileana's breasts which were outlined against the silk of her blouse and to her own annoyance she felt like blushing before she replied:

"That is none of your business! I am an inhabitant of Zokāla, and now I will return the way I came."

She rose to her feet as she spoke and Olav rose too.

She knew as he adjusted the ropes around her shoulders that he was nervous.

The Brigands, for that was what they certainly looked like, encircled them and the one who spoke Bulgarian said:

"Both come with us. Tell General why you come."

For a moment Ileana felt frightened. Then she knew that this was exactly what she had wanted.

What could be better than if she met General Vladilas and heard from him what he intended?

One thing was quite certain: He would have no idea of who she was and, if he thought her to be a boy as the Bulgarian had done, so much the better.

"I would like to meet your Leader," she said with a smile.

Then to Olav she said:

"Give me my coat."

He took it from his back and unrolled it from the muslin which his wife had wrapped round it to keep it clean.

As she was doing so Ileana shrugged off the ropes around her shoulders, aware that the men were watching her curiously.

She was certain their eyes were on her breasts, but once the coat was on and buttoned, she felt protected and she felt too that they were more likely to accept that she was a boy.

She had not worn her hat while she climbed, but her hair was pinned close to her head to prevent it from blowing in her face if there was any wind.

Now she put her sable cap on and pulled it firmly down on her forehead.

"What should we do, Gracious Lady?" Olav asked in a whisper.

"We will meet their Leader. But call me 'Sir.' They think I am a boy, and it is important that they should continue to think so."

Olav nodded as though he understood and again Ileana smiled at the Bulgarian.

"Lead the way!" she said.

He set off immediately and Ileana followed him with Olav just behind her and the rest of the men behind him.

Although it was rough going there was no need on this side for the ropes and by jumping from rock to rock and occasionally having to let themselves down by their hands they descended the mountain without any trouble.

Only as they reached the level ground and Ileana saw ahead of them one of the brilliantly coloured tents that she had seen from above did she wonder if she was walking into a hornets' nest.

At the same time she knew it was the most exciting thing that could have happened, and she was already thinking what a triumph it would be when she returned and told the Generals what she had discovered.

Now she could see to the left of her the guns drawn by the horses.

They were still exercising in the flat valley, turning in formation, proceeding first in one direction, then in the other.

Then as she looked back from where they were going she realised that the Bulgarian Brigand had reached the entrance of the tent.

It was far larger and more impressive than she had expected it to be, and she thought that perhaps because of its colour she would find that General Vladilas was decked out like some Oriental Potentate, wearing a turban and smoking a *hookah*. As she smiled at her own fantasy the Bulgarian said:

"You wait here!"

"Of course," Ileana replied and turned to look again at what was happening in the valley.

Now she could see how many guns there were drawn up on either side of what she thought of as the Parade Ground.

Automatically she began to count the men who were either sitting in the shade of the guns, or stretched out asleep under the rocks.

Those who were moving about walked with a swagger which proclaimed their sense of superiority, and what she was sure was a belief in their own invulnerability.

They were very picturesque, so fascinating that she thought, they might have stepped straight out of a fairy-tale.

Looking at them as they gazed curiously at her, she was sure that some of them were Greek, some undoubtedly Turkish, and others might have belonged to any of the other Balkan countries.

Of one thing she was absolutely certain: They were all immensely strong and undoubtedly, as the Greeks had found, magnificent fighters.

She felt a sudden sense of panic as if already she could see her soldiers being mown down by their guns.

Then as she wondered frantically what she could do she heard the Bulgarian say:

"My Leader see you. Come, please."

He made a sign as he spoke for her to enter the tent and she knew as she walked towards him that he stopped Olav from following her.

For a moment it was difficult to adjust her eyes to the darkness inside the tent after the brilliance of the sunshine outside.

Then at the far end of it she could see a man who was writing at a table.

As she walked towards him he rose to his feet. She knew that this was General Vladilas but that he was very different from what she had expected.

He was tall and broad-shouldered, and she saw at a quick glance that he was exceedingly handsome.

At the same time he had that same look of super-iority as the Bandits he commanded.

He was not dressed in a flamboyant style, but was wearing a uniform that seemed vaguely familiar, until Ileana realised with a sense of shock that it was almost identical to that worn by the officers of the Zokālan Army.

Then as she stood in front of him, wondering if she should speak or wait for him to do so, General Vladilas put out his hand and said:

"This is a surprise, Princess Ileana, but I am de-lighted to welcome you!"

chapter three

For a moment Ileana was too astonished to reply.

Then without thinking she said the first thing that came into her head.

"You know who I am?"

General Vladilas smiled before he replied:

"Of course!"

There was silence. Then he said:

"Will you sit down? I am sure after your hard climb, which I have been told you managed extremely efficiently, you would like something to drink."

He indicated as he spoke, two chairs with a low round table in front of them.

Without waiting for her answer he snapped his fingers and immediately as if he was waiting to do so, a man came in carrying a bottle of wine on a tray on which there was also two glasses.

He set it down in front of them and as he left the room Ileana could not help thinking he was behaving exactly as a trained servant in the Palace would have done.

Since the General obviously expected it, Ileana sat down on one of the chairs and because it was very hot in the tent, pushed her fur cap a little further off her forehead.

It was quite obvious that her pretence of being a boy could not be maintained.

The General, she thought looked at her searchingly, in a manner that she felt was somehow impertinent, before he seated himself at the table beside her and poured out the wine.

Because she was in fact very thirsty and, to tell the truth, more nervous than she expected to be, she sipped from the glass and found the wine was delicious with a bouquet she did not remember having tasted before.

Then because it was in her mind she said:

"It seems that somebody was watching me climb Bela. If so he was very skilfully concealed."

She thought the General smiled slightly and she added:

"There were eagles hovering overhead which led me to believe there were no look-outs."

"That is a simple trick!"

"A trick?"

"An eagle will always hover where there is a lamb or some other small animal in sight."

"That is clever!" Ileana exclaimed. "It would put many people off their guard."

As she spoke she was thinking it was the sort of thing that the Zokālan Army should know and was quite certain the Generals were in complete ignorance of such a ruse.

Then quickly, as if she must explain away her presence, Ileana said:

"I often climb Bela. It is something I greatly enjoy,

and I certainly did not expect to be more or less arrested on my own mountain!"

She had decided it would be a good thing to put him on the defensive.

Then she had the uncomfortable feeling that the General was aware of what she was intending, and the way he sat back in his chair told her he was very much at his ease.

After a moment he said:

"You are very much more beautiful near to than at a distance!"

"You have seen me before?"

"Of course!"

"What do you mean—of course?" Ileana asked. "I have not left Zokāla for over two years."

Again he smiled as if her reply was somewhat ridiculous and she asked:

"Are you telling me that you have been in my country?"

"I was there only a short time ago."

"If that is true, then why was I not informed of it?"

"There was no reason why you should be. I did not come, as you might say, as myself but incognito."

There was something in the way he spoke which made Ileana stiffen.

Then as she thought of the guns which were drawn up outside she said:

"Are you telling me that you were...spying on Zokāla?"

"That is an unattractive way of putting it," the General replied. "I was, in fact, trying to find out how well Zokāla is ruled and how efficient her defences are."

Ileana put down her glass and sat upright in her chair.

"Why should you be interested?"

The question was sharp and she knew as she spoke that it was of vital importance.

For a moment the General made no reply. Then after a pause he said:

"What I learnt on my visit or, if you prefer, on my investigation, was that Zokāla is extremely vulnerable and that any country which is interested in conquering her could do so very easily!"

He spoke slowly and clearly, and the intonation in his voice did not change from the pleasant tone in which he had spoken ever since her arrival.

Nevertheless Ileana felt her heart contract, and after a pregnant silence she said almost in a whisper:

"Is that what you . . . intend to . . . do?"

As she spoke her eyes met the General's, and there was a strange expression in his which she did not understand.

At the same time she thought that although he was undoubtedly very handsome, there was a ruthlessness about his face which made him seem very different from other men.

It certainly produced an air of authority which obviously matched his position.

She thought too there was something hard, almost

cruel, in the lines of his mouth and the squareness of his chin, and the idea came to her that he was like an eagle hovering over Zokāla waiting to strike.

"The answer to that question," he replied, "lies with you."

"With me? How is that possible?"

The General rose to his feet.

"I have something to show you," he said.

He walked towards the entrance of the tent and because there was nothing else Ileana could do, she followed him.

For a moment the blazing sunshine seemed to blind her eyes, and it was difficult to see clearly.

Then she saw that Olav was standing to one side, an anxious expression on his face, and beside him were the men who had brought them down from the mountain.

Without apology the General walked towards them, said something that she could not hear, then returned to her side.

As they walked on she was aware that Olav and the other men had turned away and she thought perhaps her guide was to be entertained and given something to drink, as she had been.

Then the General began to walk quickly towards what she thought looked like a Parade Ground.

She saw then that she had been right in thinking it was stacked on either side with guns, vehicles drawn by horses and hundreds of boxes which she was sure contained ammunition.

The men sitting about were like those she had already seen, rifles on their shoulders, long knives and pistols in their belts.

They all seemed to be tall, broad-shouldered and unusually strong.

They stared at her with curiosity, and she thought too there was a glint in their eyes which told her they were not deceived by her severe riding-coat into thinking she was a boy.

The General did not speak, he only paused occasionally in front of some special gun or another instrument of war which she did not always recognise.

It was as if he was determined she should notice everything.

They came to where the guns were still being manoeuvred up and down and the first thing Ileana thought was what fine horses were drawing them.

As if she had spoken the General said:

"I was quite certain they would please you!"

"They are magnificent!" Ileana enthused.

"And very strong," he added. "They have to be for the work they do."

It was then that Ileana looked at the guns and knew they were larger with longer barrels than any the Zokālan Army possessed.

Again the General did not speak, but walked on and she saw that on either side of a river which ran down the centre of the valley, very low at this time of year, there were dozens of horses as fine as those pulling the guns.

As if she could not help herself she exclaimed:

"Where can you have found such magnificent animals, and so many of them?"

"I brought the mares over from Arabia some years ago," the General explained.

"So they are Arab horses!"

"As I am sure you know, the fastest in the world!" he said quietly. "But there are also other breeds, which I think you will appreciate."

"Do show them to me," Ileana begged.

"I have already given orders for them to be brought in for you to see later on," the General replied, "but first, having shown you some of the material I have assembled here, I want to talk to you, and the easiest way is to return to my tent."

He spoke as if there was no point in her protesting or having any feelings of her own about it.

Turning, he started to walk back the way they had come, this time indicating and occasionally stopping to look at guns massed on the other side of the ground directly under the mountain over which she had come into the valley.

What she saw frightened her.

She was well aware without it being put into words that the General, if he wished, could take over the rest of Zokāla as easily as he had taken over the valley.

Everywhere she looked she could see his men, his guns, his vehicles, and his horses.

Looking straight ahead beyond the tents she could see that the approach to the valley which was about a mile-and-a-half away and had always been kept isolated, seemed to have changed.

She had the idea that the General had widened the pass which led to Zokāla from the South, so that it would be easier for himself and his followers to enter this part of the country.

Once again Ileana felt furious that her Army Intelligence had no idea that they were here, although they could not have moved in without taking at least two or three days to do so.

There was however no point in saying so to the General, and she began to think of all the scathing remarks she would make to the Generals when she returned to the Palace.

She would also call an emergency meeting of the Council tonight, however late it might be.

She knew there was every reason to think they were in a dangerous position even though she had never imagined such a thing could happen.

They walked back again into the tent, and as they did so Ileana said:

"I have enjoyed your hospitality, General, but you will understand that I would not wish to be late returning home in case anybody should start worrying about me. Even with Olav as a guide, the mountain can be somewhat treacherous as soon as the sun goes down."

"I am aware of that," the General replied, "and as it is already growing late you will of course, stay here as my guest."

"It is very kind of you, but I am afraid it is impossible!"

"That is a word I do not understand and is not in

my vocabulary," the General said. "If you wish to return, then of course I will send you back, but first I have a proposition that I want you to consider carefully."

Ileana smiled.

"Of course, General! I am only too willing to listen to anything you propose. At the same time, you will understand that I do not wish people to be perturbed by my absence."

The General did not reply.

He had not sat down as she had, but had remained standing.

Now, when he sat on the edge of his desk facing her she thought again he was very much at his ease and self-assured.

The desk was one that she knew Officers carried with them when they were travelling and which could be divided into three parts for packing, then joined together on arrival.

There was also an Officer's chest-of-drawers in the tent with the corners reinforced with brass to make it stronger.

On the floor was a beautiful Persian carpet which she was sure was very valuable.

It struck her that if this was the way the General lived, he certainly made himself comfortable.

Then he began to speak and she concentrated on what he was saying.

"When I came to Zokāla recently," he said, "I was quite frankly shocked at the condition of the Army."

"What do you mean by that?" Ileana asked sharply.

"The guns are out of date, the training as obsolete as the rifles, and the only thing that can be commended is the horsemanship of the Cavalry."

The General spoke so scathingly that Ileana felt her temper rising.

"That may be your opinion, General," she replied, "but we are a peaceful nation, and our neighbours are friendly towards us."

"Who told you that?" the General asked. "Your Foreign Secretary? He should have been retired years ago!"

That was something that Ileana thought herself but had not seen fit to say so, and she felt extremely annoyed to have this stranger criticising what she thought of as 'Her Government.'

In an icy voice which she could use very effectively when she wished, she said:

"It is very easy, General, to find fault. At the same time, as my father has been so ill for such a long time, I thought it would be a mistake to make too many changes."

"What you are saying," the General said, "is that you are waiting until he is dead, when you intend to take over the throne."

As this was true it was with difficulty that Ileana prevented herself from gasping at him.

Instead, still in the same cold voice, she managed to reply:

"That, General, is my business!"

"It also happens to be mine!"

"Yours?"

"Yes, mine!" he said quietly. "And this is where you have a choice."

"I do not know what you are talking about."

"Then let me make it clear! It is impossible, as I know your Statesmen have told you, for you to govern Zokāla without a husband by your side."

His lips twisted in a somewhat cynical smile as he said:

"I know you have had a great many applicants for the post, but have dismissed them all, for which I do not blame you. Each one of them would have proved completely inadequate as the type of Ruler you require."

Now Ileana did gasp and she asked:

"How can you possibly know all . . . this?"

"It is not very difficult," the General answered. "But because you have failed to give Zokāla what it so urgently needs—a King—that is why I am here!"

"I do not understand."

"Your choice is simple," the General said without moving. "You can either marry me and I will ensure the defence of Zokāla against her enemies, or else I will take over the country!"

Now Ileana gave a gasp that was perfectly audible before she said:

"You must be mad!"

"On the contrary, I am very sane and sensible."

"But we have no enemies, and although I admit the Army needs a certain amount of modernisation my soldiers would fight valiantly against any attempt on your part to conquer Zokāla."

She thought as she spoke her voice sounded very confident.

At the same time, she knew what the General's guns could do to her inadequately armed Army which had never anticipated anything as formidable as the force which was already inside the country.

As if what she was thinking showed in her green eyes the General watching her said after a moment:

"Exactly! It would be a bloody massacre unparalleled in the history of Zokāla!"

"If you think that, then why should you contemplate anything so ghastly and so wicked?"

"I have already given you an alternative. I will marry you, and the menace which now threatens you will certainly not materialise for a very long time."

"What menace?"

"You would know, if you had an effective Intelligence Service, that Hungary is being ordered by Austria to invade and take over Zokāla. In my opinion, it is only a question of months—perhaps only weeks—before that happens!"

"I do not believe you!"

"It is true! The Austrians are very ambitious."

Because of the calm way in which he spoke, what he was saying seemed more impressive and, Ileana thought, more frightening than if he had made it sound more dramatic.

Now she thought about it, she had the sneaking feeling he was right.

Thinking back, she could remember the Hungarian Ambassador the last time they had met, had not seemed as friendly as usual.

They had so much in common with their love of horses that affairs of State were often set aside and they talked of other things that most interested them both.

But she recalled now that Count Róziliki had seemed ill at ease and much more formal than he usually was.

She also thought, although it was something she could not be sure about, that he did not meet her eyes and he certainly omitted to pay her the fulsome compliments she had come to expect from him.

No Hungarian could ever resist telling her she was not only beautiful, but also the finest rider they had ever seen.

She could not believe that the reason why the Count was so reticent was that she herself had changed.

"You must be aware that Hungary has more interest in acquiring Zokāla than either Serbia or Rumania has," the General said sharply, "and unless they are prevented from doing so, they will walk in with so little opposition that it does not bear even considering!"

"Why should you think that?" Ileana asked.

"Because at least half of the men in the Zokālan Army have Hungarian blood in them, and to Hungarians the tie of blood means more perhaps then to any other country in Europe."

Even though this was true, it surprised Ileana that the General should be aware of it.

At the same time, because of the relaxed way he was sitting on the edge of his desk and the calmness of his voice, she could hardly believe that what he was saying was as frightening as it sounded.

She put down the glass she was holding in her hand and rose to her feet.

"I have been listening most carefully to everything you have been saying to me," she said, "and I think the best thing I can do is to think over what you have suggested and discuss it with my Prime Minister and the rest of the Cabinet. I will then let you have an answer as swiftly as possible, perhaps within twenty-four hours."

As she finished speaking the General laughed and it was a sharp sound that had no humour in it.

"I should be very foolish," he replied, "if now that I have you here I let you go without your making any decision."

He saw by the expression on her face that she was wondering how she could answer that, and he went on:

"I had intended to bring you here either today or tomorrow, and when you left the Palace my men were ready to ride out to intercept you."

Ileana stared at him wide-eyed as he went on:

"Then to their surprise and mine, you decided to make things very easy by climbing the mountain!"

Ileana drew in her breath.

"Are you telling me," she asked, "that you had intended to . . . kidnap me?"

"A very dramatic word for being escorted by a superior force."

"I have never heard of anything so disgraceful!" Ileana retorted. "I consider it an intolerable way of behaving, except, of course, that it is what one might expect from..."

She paused as she realised that what she had been about to say would have been rude, and that would undoubtedly be a great mistake when she was in his power.

"...what one might expect from a Brigand?" the General finished. "Of course you are right, Princess, I am a Brigand, and it is what I have been for years. At the same time, my men have their uses!"

"I hear they fought valiantly in Greece," Ileana conceded, "but then you were fighting on behalf of a throne, not against it."

"I am not fighting against one now," the General replied. "In fact, I intend to preserve the throne of Zokāla by reigning as its King, and as your husband!"

It was then that Ileana lost control of her temper which had been rising all the time they had been talking.

"I have no wish to marry anybody," she said angrily, "and certainly not you!"

The General did not move. He merely sighed before he said:

"Very well, I will take over the country by force, and there will be no question of waiting until your father's death. I will be crowned immediately and run things my own way."

"That would be a monstrous thing to do! Completely unethical and unjustified!"

"I think not. I can give you a dozen examples of very much the same thing happening all through history," the General replied, "but the situation is urgent, and I cannot afford to wait, or rather Zokāla cannot!"

"I think you are exaggerating the whole situation," Ileana argued.

"Are you prepared to take the risk?" the General enquired. "The Hungarian Army will not be as up-to-date as mine, but they could certainly make short work of your toy soldiers!"

Ileana stamped her foot.

"That is offensive and intolerable!" she stormed. "I will not stay here and listen to you any longer!"

She turned as she spoke and walked out of the tent.

She intended to find Olav and insist on returning the way they had come, but as she emerged she saw just outside the entrance several magnificent horses which she remembered the General had told her would be brought for her inspection.

Without hesitating, driven impulsively by her desire to escape, she seized hold of the saddle of the stallion opposite her and swung herself into it, almost as if she had wings.

Her action took the man who was holding it by surprise, and as she gathered the reins and moved forward he instinctively let go of the bridle and she was away.

She had already seen where the way out of the valley lay and knew it was a straight gallop with no obstacles in sight.

The stallion was obviously fresh and sprang forward as soon as she dug her heels into his sides.

Then they were off, moving at a wild gallop that

would have been thrilling and exhilarating if Ileana had not been anxious about being overtaken.

Her fear was soon substantiated, for she had not gone very far before she heard the sound of hoofs behind her and knew without turning her head who was following.

She had a start, but not a very long one, and she knew that once the General realised what she had done he had only to jump onto one of the other horses that were being paraded for her.

At the same time Ileana knew there was nobody in the whole country who could ride as well as she could, especially when she had a horse that had Arab blood in him and was superlative in every way.

She was moving so fast that she thought it would be impossible for anybody to catch up with her.

Yet as she bent lower in the saddle and urged the stallion in every way she could without having a whip in her hand, she could hear the General's horse coming nearer and nearer.

They were both moving so quickly that Ileana was not surprised when her sable cap blew from her head.

She hardly noticed it had gone, intent as she was on outriding the General and reaching the safety of the Palace.

But she could not have travelled more than half a mile before he was riding alongside her.

She tried by every means she could to prevent him from doing so, but he drew his horse nearer and nearer still, until they were so close that she felt they must collide.

Then the General performed the trick that was the

most difficult and most admired in any horseman.

While travelling at full gallop he lifted her from the saddle of her horse onto his.

As he did so Ileana could hardly believe it could have happened.

It was a feat she had seen performed only once or twice in her travels in Hungary and never thought it could happen to her.

For one second there was the feeling of flying through the air, and the next moment she landed against his chest with a thud which almost knocked her unconscious.

The General reined in his horse, turned and started to ride back with her captive across his saddle, her head on his shoulder.

Now that she had lost her sable cap, the pins fell from her head and she knew her hair was streaming over her coat glinting golden in the afternoon sun.

She heard the General give a shrill whistle above her head and knew, almost as if it was a final humiliation, that the stallion she had been riding had turned at the sound.

The General could have stopped him at any moment he wished and the stallion would have brought her back to him without any effort.

Instead he had proved his dominance and his undoubted horsemanship by carrying her back in his arms.

It was then she heard the cheers ring out from his men and knew they were cheering their Leader and his exhibition of authority over a woman who had tried to defy him.

They reached the tent, the General dismounted with her still in his arms, another clever feat, and carrying her, walked back inside.

He did not put her down, but stood holding her until Ileana opened her eyes to say:

"I hate you! I would rather die than accept you as my husband!"

"You will not die," the General replied, "but your people will. Is that what you want?"

He spoke sharply, as if she was a foolish child who did not understand the full impact of what he had been saying.

Then as she was silent, he set her down on the ground, and feeling as if her legs would not carry her, she sank down in the chair.

He filled her glass and drank from his own as if he was thirsty before he said:

"Now, let us stop playing games! I am not prepared to listen to any more nonsense. You will marry me tonight, and tomorrow we will drive into Zokāla at the head of my troops and inform our people that they are safe and protected."

"Do you really think I will . . . agree to . . . that?"

She wanted to sound firm and defiant, but even to herself she sounded ineffective.

"There is no question of whether you agree or do not agree," the General replied. "Everything is arranged, and the Priest who travels with me will be waiting for us in an hour's time."

Ileana parted her lips to say that she would refuse to do as he told her, but he went on:

"As I have no intention of marrying you wearing those clothes you have on now, you will find a Greek wedding-gown in your tent, which, since the Service will be performed by a Greek Priest, is appropriate."

"If you think I am going to change my clothes to please you, you are very much mistaken!" Ileana said defiantly.

But as she spoke, she had the terrifying feeling that the General was sapping her will and making her nothing but a puppet in his hands.

"As I intend to marry a woman and not a pseudo-boy," he said scornfully, "you will change your dress! Otherwise you will find I am quite experienced as a lady's-maid!"

There was a mocking twist to his lips which made her detest him.

Then because she was frightened she said:

"You must see this is a . . . ridiculous way to behave! Surely you must realise that I should have time to think over what is best not only for myself but also for my country?"

"I know what is best for Zokāla," the General replied, "and as I have already told you, time is something we neither of us can afford."

He walked towards one side of the tent as he said:

"Come and change, and I am sure that after all your exertions today you would like a bath."

This was true, but Ileana had no intention of admitting it and rose to her feet wondering once again if there was any possible way by which she could escape.

She was quite sure that horses would not be waiting outside a second time, and the General was standing at an opening of the tent, with an expression in his eyes that she did not like to interpret.

Holding her head high, at the same time feeling it was difficult to look dignified with her hair falling over her shoulders, she stalked past him.

She found that his tent connected with another in which there were two women who curtsied when she appeared.

One of them was obviously Greek and very beautiful, and the other was older and looked like a Bulgarian.

The General had not followed her and as the fold of the tent fell back into place and she was alone with the women, Ileana said, speaking in Greek:

"Help me! I have no wish to stay here! How can I get away?"

She felt the women looked at her in surprise as she added:

"I will reward you well if you will show me how I can escape."

The Greek woman obviously understood what she said, but at the same time she looked in consternation at the other woman as if she could hardly believe what she was hearing.

Then in a soft, musical voice she replied:

"It is impossible, Your Royal Highness, to do anything but what our Leader asks."

"Are you sure of that?"

In answer, as if it was the only way to convince

her, the woman drew aside the flap of the tent which covered the opening leading outside.

Peeping through what was only a small aperture Ileana could see two large men wearing their shaggy *shoudas* standing directly outside as if they were on sentry duty.

The Greek woman closed the flap and said:

"Your bath is ready, Your Royal Highness."

The tent had another opening at the back, and Ileana saw there was a much smaller tent attached to it.

In the centre was a large tin bath which she knew would be light enough to be carried easily in any vehicle.

It was now filled with water which to her surprise she found was scented with alpine flowers.

Because she was in fact, very hot and sticky from her climb up the mountain and her wild dash for freedom, she allowed the women to help her undress.

Only when she felt cool and clean and had dried herself on a surprisingly luxurious Turkish towel did she remember that the General had chosen a wedding-gown for her.

The impertinence of it was as infuriating as the fact that he was determined to marry her.

"How can I marry such a man?" she asked herself.

Even as every instinct within her body rebelled against the thought, she was at the same time frightened of him.

Frightened because he had already proved his physical dominance by a feat of horsemanship that she knew could not have been equalled by any man in Zokāla.

Frightened also by the manner in which he had offered her as an alternative to marrying him an inevitable massacre of her people.

"What can I do? What can I do?" she asked and knew that never in her whole life had she imagined she could find herself in such a predicament from which there appeared to be no escape.

"Perhaps the Priest will not be a genuine one," she told herself.

Then she knew that everything she had seen so far had obviously been thought out and planned down to the very last detail.

It was not likely, if he wished to be King of Zokāla, that the General would not make certain that their marriage was legal, and there would be no way out of it—except by death.

There was a brooding look in Ileana's eyes as she allowed the women to help her into the gown which she had to recognise was extremely beautiful.

She had learnt in the past that every Greek girl of every rank of society prized her wedding-gown above everything else.

She spent years embroidering and making it a feat of craftsmanship which ensured that every Greek bridal gown was not only beautiful, but also unique.

What was more, every Greek family possessed a necklace that had been handed down from mother to daughter and worn by generation after generation of brides on their wedding-day.

These were now coveted by Museums because they were so exquisite and so valuable.

The gown into which Ileana was helped was white, embroidered with brilliant-coloured flowers round the hem, on the sleeves and on the bodice.

It was so exquisite that Ileana almost forgot it was provided by the General and she could not help admiring something that was so lovely.

"It belonged to our Leader's mother," the Greek woman told her, "and we are always told she was very beautiful, Gracious Lady."

Ileana's lips trembled but there was nothing she could say.

Because she was angry she refused to admire the necklace made of precious stones that came from the mountains of Greece and was set with diamonds.

There were earrings to match, and the Greek maid parted her hair down the middle so that it waved on either side of her face, and arranged her long tresses in a chignon low on her head.

She then placed on it a Greek tiara, also of precious stones, which arched over her head rather than encircled it.

From it hung a veil which fell down the back of her gown to the ground and gave her an ethereal look.

There was a long mirror in the tent, and as Ileana looked at herself in it she had to admit that she had ceased to be the Princess Ileana of Zokāla, and had become somebody who existed only in the mind of the General.

"I hate him! I hate him for doing this to me!" she murmured.

She had a sudden impulse to tear off the clothes and ruin the gown that had belonged to his mother, and to stamp into the ground the necklace and the tiara which she knew were very valuable.

Then she told herself that no matter what she did it would not deter him from his main objective which was to make her his wife.

He had not raged at her, he had never raised his voice, and yet the way he had given her his orders made her feel it impossible to disobey him.

She knew this was what the Prince himself had said Zokāla needed.

A leader who could send out vibrations that were so magnetic, so compelling, that those who received them would do his bidding without argument.

But not a Brigand, a robber, a thief!

"I hate him! I hate him!"

She wanted to scream and cry, and wanted to throw herself to the ground and refuse to move.

But she could feel once again the strength of his arms as he had lifted her from the horse she was riding onto his.

She had known too, feeling herself almost faint as he pulled her against his chest and her breasts were hurt by the impact, that he was relentless, ruthless, and if it suited him, cruel.

She knew that if she lay crying on the floor it would not divert him in any way from making her obey him.

"I will find some way to free myself of him," she vowed.

But there was nothing she could do at the moment but go to him as he expected her to do.

She must perform her part in this mockery of a marriage, which nevertheless would make him her husband, though she felt herself shaking with fury and frustration.

Then she became aware that the women were exclaiming with each other over how beautiful she looked, and were obviously delighted with their part in dressing the bride.

Now it was almost as if the General had called from the other tent, for the Greek women moved to the opening through which she had come to them and stood waiting.

For a moment Ileana could not move, she could only try frantically to think of some means of escape, some manner by which she could get away.

But there were sentries outside and she was quite certain that the tent was securely pegged to the ground all round, and whatever she tried to do would be ineffectual and humiliating.

Once again, holding her head high, determined that he should not have the satisfaction of listening to a plea for mercy, she walked from the tent she was in into the one adjoining it.

The General was waiting for her, and now she saw that he was in the same uniform that a Zokālan would have worn in his place.

He wore a white tunic over narrow red trousers with blue stripes down the sides.

His tunic was covered with decorations, some of them bejewelled, but doubtless, Ileana thought with a curl to her lips, most of them stolen.

He might have received a medal for his part in the Greek campaign, but she was quite certain that no other country would have a Bandit, a robber and an outlaw wearing its prized decorations.

It made her more sure, because she already believed that he was an imposter and an untrustworthy rogue, that he would take advantage of any situation which would help him personally.

And this was the man to whom she was to be married! A man who was holding not only her, but also her country at gunpoint.

For a moment they just stood looking at each other.

Then the General said:

"My compliments, Your Royal Highness, and may I say you look far more beautiful as a woman than when you are pretending to be a man?"

"I do not pretend, nor do I presume to be anything I am not," Ileana said sharply.

As if he understood only too well the innuendo in her voice, she saw the smile that just twisted the corners of his lips and longed to strike him.

"Do you really intend to go through with this farce?" she asked.

"It is no farce," the General replied, "but as I feel it is somewhat of an ordeal for both of us, I suggest we have a glass of champagne which might make us feel more relaxed."

Ileana longed to refuse. At the same time she thought she needed something to sustain her.

She suddenly realised it was a long time since she had eaten breakfast and had had nothing more to eat since then.

She had not thought to take something with her as she often did when she was climbing, firstly because she had not remembered to, and secondly because she had climbed the mountain on an impulse.

Having seen all she wanted to see, she had intended to return with the information straight to the Palace.

Now thinking it would be very ignominious if she actually fainted, she accepted the glass of champagne the General offered her and was about to raise it to her lips when he said:

"I think we should propose a toast—to ourselves, and to our country!"

"*My* country!" Ileana corrected because she could not help it.

The General made a slight inclination of his head before he added:

"It shall be mine too as soon as we are married."

Ileana had always been glad until this moment that she had not had a brother who would naturally have succeeded her father.

Now she wished that she could throw it in the General's face that he would not by their marriage succeed in attaining Zokāla and he could go back to the mountains where he belonged without the spoils his evil mind was counting on.

As it was, words were useless. She drank because she really needed it, and felt as if the wine took away her weakness and made her feel strong again.

The General's eyes were on her, but she would not look at him.

She thought that if he saw the hatred she felt for him he might later be on his guard, and that would be a mistake.

The General, having finished his champagne, took her glass from her.

Then he held out his hand.

"Come," he said. "They are waiting for us to begin the ceremony!"

As he spoke he drew her towards the opening of the tent.

chapter four

OUTSIDE the scene had changed since Ileana had last seen it.

Now dusk had fallen and night had come quickly as it always did in that part of the world.

The stars were shining over the peaks of the mountains and the moon was moving up the sky.

Ileana knew that as it rose higher in a short while the peaks of Bela and the other mountains would be turned to silver.

What now held her attention however was that the whole tribe was gathered in a huge circle.

For the first time she realised that not only the men had come with the General to the mountains, but they had brought their women and in some cases their children.

Everybody was dressed in what Ileana was certain was their best, and the women made brilliant patches of colour wearing native costumes with head-dresses of flowers and ribbons that contrasted with their dark hair.

In the centre of the circle Ileana saw there was an improvised altar covered with a gold cloth and on it stood a cross and a great number of lighted candles.

The Priest stood waiting wearing the vestments of the Greek Church, and with his long beard he looked not only impressive, but also she thought, convincingly authentic.

To her surprise, as the General drew her forward holding her hand, they were received in silence.

Then she realised that the ceremony which was to take place was, for those watching, as sacred as if they were in a Cathedral.

Because she had a keen appreciation of beauty, angry though she was, she could not help approving of the exquisite setting in which she was to be married.

With the mountains towering above them, the valley stretching away into an indefinable shadow and the stars overhead, the lighted candles on the altar were the focus of everybody's attention.

Somebody—she thought it was a child—put a bouquet into her hands and she saw it was made up of alpine flowers and echoed those which ornamented her gown.

As she took it without thinking her fingers tightened on the General's and as he did the same she thought he was telling her that she was his captive, as surely as if he had taken her in battle.

They walked over the dry ground until they stood in front of the Priest.

Ileana was aware there was a carpet in front of the altar and on it two velvet stools.

The Service began and because she knew what took place in a Greek Church was very like the services she attended in the Cathedral next to the Palace, she knew what to expect.

The long prayers came to an end while crowns were held over their heads by two of the Bandits.

Finally the moment came when the General put a ring on her finger and she wondered as he did so, if with his eye for detail he had, doubtless by some means of his own, found out the size of her finger.

She heard him say the words in Greek that bound them to each other for the rest of their lives, and she thought scornfully that though the idea might suit him, she would somehow eventually be rid of him.

They knelt in front of the Priest and when he had blessed them, the General drew her to her feet and those who had been watching them rose too.

To Ileana's surprise, they broke their silence by singing the Zokālan National Anthem.

They sang it spontaneously and whole-heartedly, so that the music of their voices swept up into the night and seemed to touch the very peaks of the mountains.

She realised as they sang that they must know the song well, and wondered if the General had rehearsed them.

Because it was so unexpected and also because it told her how confident he had been of becoming ruler of her country, she hated him all the more.

When it was finished, the General took her hand in his and raised it to his lips.

She wanted to snatch it from him, but he held it too tightly for her to do so.

As she felt his mouth hard and insistent on the softness of her skin, her eyes blazed at him.

Those watching took the kiss as a signal for them to break out in cheers that echoed and re-echoed round the valley.

They cheered triumphantly until the General, having bowed to the Priest while Ileana genuflected, still holding her hand, led her back into the tent.

As they went children ran in front of them scattering petals of flowers and only when they had stepped inside and vanished from view did the cheering stop.

Roughly Ileana pulled her hand away.

She wanted to say something rude and scathing, but it was impossible to declare that the Service in which they had just taken part was anything but unusual and impressive.

The General walked to the table on which stood the bottle of champagne from which they had drunk a toast before the ceremony.

He filled up their glasses and handing one to her said:

"Let me congratulate you! You came through that with flying colours!"

Ileana did not answer. She merely sipped the champagne as if she needed its sustenance.

The General having also drunk said:

"We must now wait while they prepare a banquet, and I imagine as you must by now be hungry that you will not be too particular."

"I admit to looking forward to having something to eat," Ileana replied.

The General smiled.

"You must forgive me if I forgot that you would

be used to having a meal in the middle of the day. When we are travelling, I and my people eat only at dawn and at night, and it has become a habit."

Ileana thought this was a sensible idea, but she had no intention of saying so. Instead she said:

"I suppose you realise by now that they will have become very concerned and agitated about me at the Palace."

"I anticipated that," the General replied. "So when I sent Olav back the way he had come I told him to inform your *Aides-de-Camp* that you would be returning tomorrow and that they would receive orders as to how we are to be received early tomorrow morning."

"And you think they will understand that sort of message sent by you?" Ileana enquired.

"I should have thought it was quite clear," the General replied, "but as I have already said, the instructions I will send ahead of us will be in writing, and the Prime Minister is supposed to be an intelligent man."

"You are sending instructions to my Prime Minister?" Ileana gasped. "How dare you do such a thing without consulting me!"

"What I am asking is nothing very revolutionary," the General replied, "and we have naturally to announce our marriage to our people. It would be extremely boring to do it more than once."

"I can see exactly what you are doing," Ileana exclaimed. "Having married me you think you can push me on one side, and that I will be a complacent wife tending the home and leaving the Affairs of State to you! You are mistaken! I have no intention of allowing you, even if you have taken over my country, to take me over as well!"

She seemed almost to spit the words at him and her green eyes had a glint of fire in them which echoed the lights of her hair.

The General looked at her for a long moment before he said:

"You look very much like a tiger-cat when you speak to me like that! I shall be interested to see if the fire in your eyes can be engendered by anything except hatred."

The inference was obvious and Ileana retorted:

"Not where you are concerned!"

"Some day," the General said slowly, "you must tell me about the ardent young Princes who have laid their hearts at your feet and how skilfully they made love."

Ileana knew as he spoke that he was mocking her, and it was only with the greatest effort at self-control that she prevented herself from screaming at him.

Instead she said with what she hoped was a contemptuous note in her voice:

"My feelings are my own, and certainly no concern of yours!"

He raised his eyebrows.

"I should have thought, as your husband, they were very much my concern. But this conversation, fascinating though it may be, must wait, for I think by now our wedding-feast will be waiting for us,"

As he spoke the flaps of the tent were drawn back

and as he held out his hand to her there was nothing Ileana could do but rise to her feet and accompany him.

Now the scene had changed again dramatically.

The altar had vanished and instead in front of them was a table covered by a white table-cloth decorated with flowers and set with china and cutlery in the same manner as if they were dining at the Palace.

The crowd around them were, Ileana saw, to eat where they sat and the scene was lit not only by the moon and the stars but by huge torches flaring up into the sky.

They seemed to stretch a long way into the valley, and now that she could see them clearly she thought there were even more men than she had supposed at first.

There were many hundreds of them, but while they seated themselves, the women and children were standing, ready to wait on them.

Although that was customary, Ileana's lips curled as she thought that if that was what the General would expect from her, he was very much mistaken.

They sat down at the table on chairs that were not only comfortable but were made from the horns of wild animals and were in consequence extremely decorative.

As soon as they were seated there was the sound of music and Ileana saw standing a little way from them there was a band of Gypsies playing their violins and various strange instruments.

Despite her anger, the music which she had known

and loved all her life seemed to raise her heart.

Then as the feast began she realised the wine was being poured into magnificent golden goblets set with jewels, such as she had not expected to find in the possession of a Brigand and a robber.

"Doubtless they have been stolen from some wretched nobleman who was too weak to resist him!" she told herself scornfully.

At the same time the wine was delicious, golden and mellow, and she had to admit better than anything they could produce in Zokāla.

As if he knew what she was thinking the General said:

"I thought you would enjoy this wine. It comes from a very special grape that I intend to introduce into Zokāla. I think it would do well in this valley if the soil is prepared for it."

Ileana was silent.

She was thinking, as she had before, that she had been remiss in not having the Bela Valley, as it was called, cultivated, and that in so small a country it had been a mistake to leave any land wild and unproductive.

As dish succeeded dish, each one was more delicious than the last, and although she had no wish to make herself pleasant to the man beside her she found it impossible not to ask:

"Do you always when you are travelling, eat as well as this?"

"Why not?" he asked. "I dislike discomfort for discomfort's sake. At times, naturally, especially in the winter when the snow is deep, food is scarce. But my men are skilful hunters and I make certain that what they provide is not wasted by bad cooking."

This was something Ileana had not expected in a Brigand, and she had to admit that even though she loathed the General he was obviously an educated man who appreciated comfort and elegant living.

But if so, why had he chosen such a way of life?

How, even as a General, a rank he had doubtless given himself, could he ever understand the complexities of Kingship?

"I cannot allow him to take my father's place," Ileana told herself.

At the same time she coveted the guns she could see behind them in the shadows, and even more the horses which were loose in the fields on either side of the river.

It was from the river that the fresh trout had come which she had eaten first, with a sauce which she knew contained herbs that came from the mountains, but were hard to recognise.

There was baby lamb, so tender that it melted in the mouth and a partridge cooked as only the Hungarians, to whom it was a very special game-bird, could cook it.

When Ileana felt she could eat no more, there was a dish of wild strawberries which had just ripened and with them some strange mountain berries that were more delicious than anything she had ever tasted before.

It made her angry to think that, good though the

food was in the Palace, if she was honest what she had eaten tonight surpassed anything produced by the Chefs she had always thought were the most skilful available.

The food the men were eating as they sat around them, many of them cross-legged, was, she was sure, just as good as theirs.

She knew that their strength and fitness was due to their being well-fed and obviously led in a manner which saved them from unnecessary privation.

But if the General's purpose was to show her how efficient he was, she told herself she would not be deceived.

"If he intended to impress me, he has failed!"

To finish the meal there was Turkish coffee served in the traditional handleless cups, held in gold and jewelled containers, and the pot from which the coffee was poured would be, Ileana recognised, the delight of any connoisseur.

'It is stolen! Of course it is stolen!' she thought scornfully.

Nevertheless she accepted a second cup of coffee.

Now the table in front of them was whisked away as if by magic, and into the centre of the circle came the Gypsies.

It was then the soft melody which had sounded entrancing while they were eating changed to the wild and exhilarating music to which the Gypsies danced.

The dancers came from the darkness into the light, their tambourines in their hands, the small gold bells which encircled their ankles ringing as they moved.

Ileana had seen many Gypsy dances, though her father and mother had not approved of her doing so.

Only since her father's illness had she been able to go openly to where they were camping to ask them to dance for her.

What she was seeing now was very different and she knew that the Gypsies must belong to a very superior tribe. She guessed that many of the women dancers were Russian, who were the best in the world.

Their grace was indescribable: the ease in which they leapt high into the air seeming almost to fly and their poise when they lifted their arms were worthy of any professional Ballerina.

As the great throng of Brigands swayed to the rhythm of the violins and the dancers grew wilder and wilder, Ileana was aware that without her noticing the General had left her side.

His strangely constructed chair was empty, and she wondered if this meant there was a possibility of her escaping.

But when she thought of it she knew it was impossible.

There was no sign of any horse to carry her, and she was no longer on the edge of the circle as she had been at first.

The Bandits had closed in behind, and now she was as much the focus of their eyes as the Gypsies who were dancing.

"My time will come later," she told herself reassuringly.

Then there was a sudden cheer which surprised her.

As she turned her head wondering what had specially pleased the audience, she realised that the General had returned and now he looked very different.

He was wearing black, tight-fitting trousers, a white shirt with huge embroidered sleeves, and a bolero hung with gold coins that she thought, although she was not sure, was worn by every Greek bridegroom.

There was a red satin sash tied tightly around his waist into which were thrust the knives and pistol that all Brigands wore.

His were heavily jewelled, the diamonds, rubies and emeralds glinting in the light from the torches.

As he stepped into the circle where the Gypsies were performing the women ran towards him, and as they took him by the hand he began to dance with them.

"He is certainly showing off!" Ileana murmured scornfully.

Then she had to admit that he danced as well as any Gypsy.

Never had she imagined that a man so large and so muscular could be so light on his feet, or that he could fling himself into the air with the same expertise that had been part of Gypsy dancing since the beginning of time.

She knew his followers appreciated it, for they clapped and shouted and cheered and once again their voices were ringing out to fill the whole valley with their enthusiasm.

"I hate him!" Ileana said beneath her breath.

At the same time she found it impossible not to

watch him and to watch too the women who enticed him with every gesture of their bodies, by the way they lifted their dark eyes to his and their arms reached out to touch him.

They danced until as if at a signal which Ileana did not hear the Bandits rose and began to dance too.

Then the music changed into what she thought must be a folk-dance that she had never heard before, but came perhaps from the South or from Greece.

The Bandits certainly knew every step of it and as they danced they sang, and the rhythmic motion of so many men and the enjoyment evident in their voices was in its way very moving.

Then as she sat watching, feeling a little out of it, the General was standing in front of her and, taking her by the hand, drew her to her feet.

For a moment she thought he was going to ask her to dance with him and was ready to refuse.

She knew that although she was considered to be a very good dancer in traditional style she could not equal the grace and the wild abandonment of the Gypsies.

But the General merely drew her away towards the tent and because there was no possibility of making themselves heard above the noise, they walked in silence.

Her head was aching and as they entered the tent Ileana pulled off her head-dress.

Only when she was inside did she realise that she was not in the General's tent as she had expected to be, but in her own.

She had hardly noticed the couchlike bed that had been pushed to one side while she dressed.

Now she saw it was pulled into the centre and there was a candelabrum holding three candles on one side of it and on the other a huge vase filled with flowers that scented the whole tent with their fragrance.

There were white fur rugs on either side of the bed which Ileana suddenly realised with a constriction of her heart was big enough for two.

It was then she turned her face to look at the General and realised he was closing the flap of the tent behind them and fastening it with knots which she would find it difficult to undo should she try to escape.

He bent down to fasten the one closest to the ground, and as he did so one of the jewelled daggers he wore in his sash slipped out.

With a swiftness engendered by fear Ileana picked it up.

Even as she grasped the handle the General straightened himself and turned to face her.

She backed away from him until she was standing against the bed and now she raised the dagger, the point very sharp, towards him.

"Are you defending yourself or intending to kill me?" he asked.

It was perhaps the note of amusement in his voice which made her lose the last semblance of her self-control.

While she had watched him dancing and was forced to admire the way he performed, she had felt her hatred grow.

He had not only compelled her to marry him, but also left her side without apology or explanation as if, now that he had got his way, she was of no consequence and of little further interest.

In fact, that was what she told herself she wanted, but still it infuriated her.

Now because he goaded her she replied:

"Both! I will kill you sometime, and if you touch me or come near me, I will do it now!"

"So we know exactly where we stand!" the General said calmly. "But I think while you appear very threatening you have omitted to consider what is behind you."

Involuntarily, without consciously thinking, Ileana turned her head and only as he moved did she realise that she had been caught by a very old trick.

Moving with the swiftness of a beast of prey, he grasped her wrist, forcing her hand which held the knife upwards, and at the same time bending her backwards onto the bed.

Then he was lying on top of her, pinning her down, rendering her completely helpless.

She gave a cry of unbridled terror.

At the same time, she knew how foolish she had been to let him trick her, which made her even angrier.

Slowly his fingers tightened on her wrist until as the blood drained from her hand she was forced to relinquish her hold on the knife, and it fell down on to the ground.

She was now completely at his mercy and his

expression was, she thought, triumphant as he said mockingly:

"You are not a very skilful opponent!"

"I hate you!" Ileana said. "I loathe and detest you! Leave me . . . alone!"

"And if I will not, what will you do about it?"

She felt that his weight on top of her was intolerable. One arm where he grasped it just above the elbow was extremely painful, and the fact that his fingers still held her wrist made her want to scream.

He looked down at her, and she was aware that his mouth was not far from hers, and there was an expression in his eyes that frightened her.

Quite suddenly she was afraid in a way she had never been afraid before.

She was no longer a Princess fighting a Brigand, but a woman fighting a man.

The struggle had become one which was entirely primitive, and her anger was replaced by a sickening feeling of weakness as she realised she was helpless in his power.

She was terribly afraid of what he might do, and she knew that nothing she could say could prevent him from making her his, if that was what he insisted on.

"No . . . No . . . No!"

Her voice was low and hoarse.

Without her being aware of it, her green eyes looking up into his no longer had the fire of hatred or defiance in them.

Instead there was an involuntary appeal for mercy and the look of a child who is suddenly afraid of the dark and has no idea what to do about it.

For a long time, it seemed almost a century, the General looked at her, and she felt in a strange and inexplicable way, that he was looking deep into her very heart and soul.

Then he said, and there was a note of laughter in his voice:

"I find it difficult to decide whether, since you are so unpredictable, I should beat you or kiss you!"

With an effort because he had made her breathless Ileana replied:

"If I have a...choice I would rather you...beat me...It is what I would...expect of a...Brigand."

She tried to speak in the defiant voice she had used earlier, but instead it was a soft and rather incoherent effort.

The General laughed.

"I will in future remember your preference."

He lifted himself off her, leaving her for a moment spread-eagled, her gown crumpled by the weight of his body.

Then as he stood looking down at her, she hastily sat up and straightened her dress in a protective gesture.

He moved towards his own tent and as he reached the opening he said:

"Sleep well, Ileana! Remember you are well guarded, and it would be useless for you to attempt to leave without my permission."

He did not wait for her reply, but passed into his own tent and she thought as he fastened the flap behind him that her prison was complete.

For a moment, in relief that what she had feared had not transpired and he had let her go, she felt too weak to move and lay back against the pillows.

Then she told herself that the sooner she tried to sleep the more alert she would be tomorrow to try to extract some kind of sanity out of the incredible mess in which she found herself.

It was hard to believe that only this morning she had been content, happy and safe in her own Palace, running Zokāla in her own way and determined not to be pressured into marriage by anything the Prime Minister or anybody else might say.

But now she was married—married to a Brigand, an outlaw—a man she hated with every fibre of her being, and at the same time feared.

How could this have happened? How was it possible?

Then she knew it was because he was clever enough to have such modern up-to-date weapons and so many men under his command.

However much she loathed him, she knew he was cultured enough to appreciate comfort and good food and wine, and the dancing of the Gypsies.

At the same time he was more frightening and more menacing than she had ever imagined any man could be.

"What can I do? Oh, God, what can I do?" she asked aloud.

Then because she was exhausted by all that had happened and by the turbulence of her emotions, which were far more violent than anything she had ever felt before, she knew the sensible thing to do was to go to bed.

Slowly she undressed, thinking vaguely as she did so that this had obviously been the General's sleeping tent before he had handed it over to her.

He certainly made himself very comfortable, as she found when she got into bed and appreciated the fine linen sheets beneath the lambs'-wool blankets that were as light and luxurious as anything she had in the Palace.

She knew the mattress was filled with down, as were the pillows.

When she lay down and felt as if she floated on a cloud she admitted to herself that the General, had she not been so terrifyingly involved with him, was a re-markable character and any country in which he lived would make him into a legend.

"If only I had a hundred men like him in Zokāla!" she murmured.

There was no answer to this and as she shut her eyes she felt herself drifting away into the realms of sleep where she was listening to the Gypsy music.

They were still playing outside and she thought, although it seemed impossible, the music seemed to hold out a note of hope in its wild ecstatic rhythm.

It was like a light in what was otherwise a sea of darkness, hatred and despair.

* * *

Ileana awoke to the realisation that there was some-body in her tent.

As she half-opened her eyes she saw it was the Greek woman who was picking up her wedding-gown which she had thrown carelessly down to the ground when she had taken it off the night before.

She then lifted the necklace from the table which also supported the mirror.

When she saw that Ileana was awake the Greek woman said:

"A beautiful morning, Gracious Lady! I will bring you breakfast in a few minutes. Our Leader wishes you to be ready in one hour."

"And I suppose I have to obey his order!" Ileana told herself, but she did not say so aloud.

Instead, almost as if the Greek woman compelled her, she went into the bathroom and found the bath had been refilled and was waiting for her.

The water was cool, but exhilarating.

She dried herself and came back into the bedroom to find that her breakfast was waiting on a tray.

She was relieved to find that she did not have to take this meal with the General.

Sitting still wrapped only in the big Turkish towel, she ate eggs and ham which were well cooked, and drank a cup of French coffee.

She might easily have been in her own Palace, or any other Palace in which she had stayed in the past.

But the truth was she was in the tent of a Brigand who had invaded her country unlawfully and had forced her to become his wife without giving her any chance of refusing him.

As she felt stronger, once again her anger began rising within her.

When she had finished her breakfast she rose still wrapped in the towel to look for her clothes.

She saw instead the Greek woman bringing into the tent a red skirt and a white blouse, and with them a black velvet bodice such as was traditionally worn by the native women of Zokāla.

"I want my own clothes!" she said sharply. "Where are they?"

"They are gone, Gracious Lady."

"Gone? What do you mean—gone?"

"Our Leader ordered them last night to be burnt!"

"Burnt?"

Ileana's exclamation was shrill.

"Yes, burnt," the Greek woman repeated. "Our Leader does not approve of ladies wearing clothes that are intended for men."

Ileana thought it was what she might have expected.

At the same time, the manner in which he had disposed of her belongings made her wish she had been quick enough last night to kill him when she had the opportunity.

Had she driven the knife into his back, things would now be very different.

Then she had to admit that if she had in fact, killed their Leader the Brigands would doubtless have killed her.

She was aware that he had an air of authority about him, and a kind of magnetic force which made his men follow him loyally wherever he might lead them.

'The Devil has the same power!' she thought and decided that was what he was—a Devil—and there was no doubt that he would drag her down to Hell.

Quickly, because there was nothing else she could do and she was afraid if she refused to put on the clothes the General might, as he had threatened, constitute himself a lady's-maid, she dressed herself.

First there was a lace-trimmed chemise which was silk and felt very soft on her skin.

Then she put on the stiff lace-trimmed petticoats which went under the red skirt.

As she did so she realised that the clothes were of the finest quality, and that they fitted her.

She could not but recognise the General's brilliant organising ability.

But she pressed her lips together to prevent herself from telling the Greek woman exactly what she thought of her Leader.

Then there was the blouse which was very similar to those the peasants wore, but embroidered very elaborately and edged on the large puffed sleeves with lace that was the finest made by any of the Zokālan lace-makers.

The skirt fitted exactly round her small waist and when the Greek woman placed the black velvet bodice around her, Ileana knew that the costume was exceedingly becoming.

There was an apron, also beautifully embroidered

and elaborate like those the Zokālan women kept for very special occasions.

It infuriated Ileana to know that not only the white stockings but also the black shoes, which were of leather with silver buckles, fitted her exactly.

As she sat in front of the mirror the Greek woman brushed her hair until it shone like sunlight and then as was traditional, left it hanging over her shoulders and down to her waist.

Over it she placed a wreath that arched over her head and was decorated with flowers and ribbons of green, silver and gold.

She guessed, and it annoyed her, that the General had carefully precluded there being any red near her hair.

Now she was ready and as she rose to her feet the Greek woman said:

"The Gracious Lady is very beautiful and a very fitting wife for our Leader!"

She paused. Then she said in a soft voice:

"Please, be kind to him. He is so very wonderful!"

There was something in the way she spoke and the suspicion of tears in her eyes that made Ileana look at her sharply.

She realised as she did so, how immensely beautiful the Greek woman was, almost like a goddess.

Before she could really formulate it, the idea flashed through her mind, as she remembered the way the Gypsy girls had danced with him, that his life had not been without women.

Without really understanding what she was thinking, she replied to the Greek woman sharply:

"Why should I be kind to a man who has forced me against my will to become his wife?"

"He could marry anybody he chose—anybody!" the Greek woman answered. "But he wanted you! You must, Gracious Lady, thank God on your knees for such a privilege!"

The way she spoke and the rapt note in her voice checked the angry retort that came to Ileana's lips.

Instead, feeling this was a conversation that should not have taken place, she said:

"What is your name?"

"Thelia."

"Thank you, Thelia, for looking after me. You have been very kind."

The Greek woman did not reply. She merely curtsied with her eyes downcast and her lashes long and dark against her pale cheeks.

Ileana was certain she was hiding her tears, as she turned away abruptly and without looking back walked from her tent into the adjoining one.

It was empty not only of people but of the desk and everything else with which it had been furnished yesterday.

Then as she stood wondering what she should do, the General came in through the main entrance.

"You are ready?" he asked.

His eyes flickered over her appearance almost as if he was checking to see that she was dressed exactly as he had wished her to be.

It was then she saw that he was wearing the red tunic and colourful insignia of the Commander-in-Chief of the Zokālan Army.

Under his arm he carried a plumed hat which only her father would have worn when he took the salute at the Ceremony of the Trooping the Colour.

His coat blazed with the decorations he had worn last night when he married her, and across his chest was a blue ribbon and from which dangled the jewelled decoration of St. Miklös, the Patron Saint of Zokāla.

Ileana stared at him in astonishment. Then she asked:

"How dare you deck yourself out with decorations to which you are not entitled? Even our lowest peasant will be aware that you have stolen them!"

"That is what I expected you to think," the General replied, "but explanations will be made later. Come, everything is ready for our drive into the next valley with our troops behind us. The rest of my people will follow."

For a moment Ileana defied him. Then she said:

"I am ashamed...deeply ashamed and humiliated to be associated with an imposter. One day, make no mistake, I will have my revenge!"

The General laughed.

"I shall be looking forward to it!" he replied. "But for the moment I find it somewhat early in the morning for dramatics!"

The way he spoke made Ileana clench her fingers together to prevent herself from attempting to kill him with her bare hands.

Then realising how helpless she was, she preceded him out of the tent feeling as if even the sunshine was mocking her.

chapter five

To her astonishment, Ileana saw waiting for them the Landau which her father used on State occasions.

It was an open carriage drawn by six perfectly matched white horses and the postilions accompanying it were dressed in the Royal uniform.

A Troop of the King's Cavalry were drawn up behind it, and as she and the General appeared the Officer-in-Charge saluted them.

In a voice that only the General could hear Ileana said beneath her breath:

"I suppose you ordered this in my name!"

"Of course!" he replied. "But the decorations were done by my people, and I hope you appreciate them."

Once again he was mocking her, and with her lips set in a hard line she looked coldly at the flowers on the horses' bridles, the wreaths around their necks, and the back of the Landau which was massed with flowers of every colour.

It was very attractive and picturesque but Ileana thought she could not imagine anything more humiliating than to drive to the Palace accompanied by a man who by his very appearance was, she felt, sneering at the position she occupied in Zokāla.

There was however nothing she could do but step into the Landau, and they drove off cheered by those of the Bandits and their followers who were not taking part in the procession.

She was well aware that behind the Cavalry had been lined up the General's huge guns, and because she could not repress her curiosity she looked back as they turned out of the Bela valley to see the enormous procession she was heading which seemed to stretch away indefinitely.

Once on the main road the horses could travel faster, and Ileana knew it would not take more than about an hour-and-a-half to reach the Palace.

She imagined she could see it in the far distance ahead of her and thought how different her feelings had been the previous morning when she had left it intending only to find out from Olav how much he knew about the Pallikares.

Never in her wildest imagination had she thought she would return married to their Leader—a man she despised, and of whom at the same time, she was afraid.

She would not look at him as he sat beside her, wearing the plumed hat which could only be worn by the Commander-in-Chief of the Army.

She thought he was positively inviting the citizens of Zokāla to expose, imprison and even execute him for his impertinence.

At the same time, whatever she might feel about him personally, she knew that the long line of guns following them was very impressive.

Even the stupidest Zokālan would know they were

an effective and welcome answer to the ambitions Hungary or any other country might have of conquering them.

As soon as they reached the centre of the valley where the peasants were working in the fields their appearance evoked a great deal of excitement and the men and women came running to the roadside.

As soon as they saw Ileana they burst into cheers, and were obviously exceedingly curious as to who was sitting beside her in the State Landau.

The General acknowledged their cheers with salutes, and as they drew nearer to the City the crowds lining the route grew thicker.

"I think," the General remarked, breaking a long silence between them, "that seeing how you are dressed, they suspect you are now the bride they hoped for."

Ileana thought he was mocking her.

"Bride of a Brigand!" she replied bitterly.

"As you say," he agreed.

Looking at him she saw he was smiling agreeably and she hated him more than ever.

The news of their coming must have sped ahead of them to the City, and Ileana was not surprised to find really dense crowds by the time they halted at the outside walls.

What did surprise her however was that once inside the horses did not turn, as she expected, towards the Palace, but carried straight on.

In mingled curiosity and indignation she found herself obliged to ask:

"Where are we going?"

"To the Market Square," he answered, "where you have ordered your Prime Minister and Cabinet to meet us on the steps of the House of Parliament."

"Did you say *I* ordered them!" she remarked sarcastically.

"I was merely anticipating your wishes."

"I am sure they will be grateful for your guns if they are to be used in the defence of Zokāla!" Ileana said, "but I cannot imagine that either socially or politically a Brigand and a robber would be welcome as my husband!"

He laughed as if at the sharp note in her voice before he replied:

"I am looking forward to surprising you."

"You have already done that enough to last me a lifetime!" Ileana retorted.

"I hope not. I would find life very dull if I did not see your green eyes flashing and your lips spitting hatred, when really they were meant for kisses!"

Ileana stiffened.

At the same time, because what he said was so surprising, it infuriated her to know that the colour was rising in her cheeks.

"I think, if we are speaking frankly to each other," the General went on, "you will find both your Cabinet and your people will enjoy seeing you as the personification of beauty, looking exactly how every Zokālan dreams a Zokālan woman should look."

Because the General, having burnt her own clothes and dressed her like a puppet, seemed again to be taunting her, Ileana wanted to tear her wreath from her head and throw it at him.

But the carriage was already moving through the crowds who were cheering and waving.

Flowers were being thrown into the carriage and women were wishing her 'Good Luck,' almost as if they knew she was married—or perhaps in love.

Then as the horses moved slowly through the packed throng in the Market Square she saw the Prime Minister and the Members of the Cabinet standing at the top of the flight of steps which led into the House of Parliament.

She knew they must be wondering what had happened, and were undoubtedly bewildered by the orders they presumably had received very early in the morning.

But they were there, and as the carriage drew nearer to them Ileana could not help feeling they were all very old.

There was something tired and dispirited about these elderly and middle-aged men, and she knew they were a startling contrast to the youth, vitality and magnetism of the man sitting beside her.

The carriage came to a standstill, the servants rolled down a red carpet, and the bodyguard took up their positions, one at the end of each step.

A flunkey opened the carriage door.

The General stepped out and put out his hand to help Ileana alight. She tried to avoid touching him but his fingers closed over hers.

Then as they started to walk slowly and with dignity

up the steps the carriage drove away.

As they reached the top the Prime Minister stepped forward to say:

"It is a very great honour, Your Royal Highness, to receive you at the House of Parliament and my colleagues join me in welcoming your distinguished guest."

As he spoke Ileana thought his eyes flickered for a moment over the Blue Ribbon of the Order of St. Miklös and the other decorations worn by the General.

There was a little pause when Ileana knew she should present the man beside her. But somehow the words would not come to her lips, and without waiting for her to find her voice the General held out his hand, saying:

"I am delighted to meet you, Prime Minister, and now, on behalf of myself and Her Royal Highness the Princess Ileana, I have a statement to make, and I hope you will allow me to make it from here."

The Prime Minister was obviously taken aback, but there was nothing he could reply except to say after a glance at Ileana:

"If that is the wish of Her Royal Highness."

The General shook hands with the rest of the Council and while he was doing so chairs were hastily brought and placed on the top of the steps which made a natural platform.

Ileana seated herself in the centre, and having completed his greetings the General turned round to face the curious and excited throng of people in the Market Square.

Looking at them, Ileana thought she had never before seen so many Zokālans gather in one place.

She realised as she looked that while the Troop of Cavalry had followed them into the Market Place the guns were being grouped in an orderly formation on level ground just in front of the Palace.

It was where parades always took place, but she was surprised that the General should be aware of this.

Then she told herself bitterly that he had obviously spied out the land so efficiently that he would know exactly what to do and would make no mistakes.

At the same time, as he stood in front of her, looking down at the great sea of faces staring up at him, she had to admit that he looked impressive, even though it might be a mockery that he was in fancy-dress.

Then his voice rang out and it was, as she expected, so strong and resolute that she was sure even the youths who had climbed the trees at the far end of the Market Place could hear every word.

"People of Zokāla," he began, "I bring you the glad tidings that yesterday Her Royal Highness the Princess Ileana and I were married in the beautiful valley of Bela!"

For a second there was silence, then a gasp of astonishment, before cheers broke out.

They cheered and cheered until the General turned back and taking Ileana by the hand drew her forward so that they could acknowledge the cheers side by side.

He then took her back to her seat and putting up his hand for silence said:

"Thank you for that delightful expression of good

will. Now I want to introduce myself, and I think that some of the older citizens here today will remember my father."

He paused, and it seemed almost as if nobody in the crowd breathed before he continued:

"I am Prince Vladilas, only son of His Royal Highness Prince Alexander of Zokāla."

There was a burst of applause, and again the General silenced them before he continued:

"My father and King Milko were first cousins, and my father lived in the family Castle in the West of our country which borders on Rumania. Unfortunately, althouth the two young men were at first very close friends, they quarrelled soon after they had both come of age. As they were Zokālans, you will understand that inevitably the quarrel involved a beautiful woman!"

There was a roar of laughter at this but Ileana felt that the people, like herself, were listening breathlessly to everything he had to say.

"Finally," the General went on, "their estrangement became so violent that King Milko ordered my father to leave the country. It was an order, I am sure, he did not expect to be obeyed. But proudly my father left Zokāla, saying that never again would he return to a land that did not want him."

There was a cry at this from some of the women and the General remarked:

"You are right! In a way it broke my father's heart, but at the same time no Zokālan, as you well know, will allow himself to be humiliated, and it is something that must never happen to us."

The General glanced down at the people listening to him before he went on:

"My father travelled in many countries until finally he married a Greek Princess who was the embodiment of beauty, charm and sweetness, and I only wish you could have known her.

"Then I was born, and as I grew up, I began to long for the country to which I belonged, and which I knew, although he would never admit it, was always in my father's mind."

There was something very moving in the way he spoke and Ileana saw that the whole Cabinet were leaning forward in their chairs listening intently.

"I have no time now to tell you how many countries I visited as I grew older," the General continued, "or in how many battles I was involved in one way or another, both in my mother's country, and in others."

His voice deepened and at the same time grew louder as he said:

"It was only when I learnt a year or so ago that Zokāla was in danger of being conquered by one of her neighbours that I knew I had to save her and provide her with the modern weapons which were essential if she was to survive.

"My father, before he died, knew what I intended to do, and as he gave me his blessing he said:

"'You must save Zokāla and when you reign over her, as I should do if I lived to survive King Milko who has no son, wear my decorations as well as your own because they are to me the most precious treasures I possess.'"

As he finished speaking Prince Vladilas threw out his arms and said:

"In the name of my father and as the husband of your future Queen, I ask you to accept me as your Leader, your Ruler, and the Saviour of this country which we all love!"

The response was deafening.

The people cheered, jumped up and down, waved their handkerchiefs, their hats and their sticks.

There was in fact, a demonstration of such spontaneous joy and excitement that Ileana felt the tears come into her eyes because it was so moving.

The Cabinet had risen to their feet and were clapping and cheering as if they too could not restrain themselves.

Once again Prince Vladilas turned to Ileana and brought her forward to stand beside him.

Because Ileana was very popular with the people, the sight of her made the cheers increase in volume until they were completely deafening.

Then, as he had done the night before, Prince Vladilas raised Ileana's hand to his mouth and once again she felt his lips warm and insistent upon her skin.

Now the Prime Minister was indicating that they should go inside the building and as they did so Ileana asked in a whisper:

"Why did you not tell me?"

Prince Vladilas smiled before he replied:

"I wanted to surprise you. You must forgive me if you feel you have been deceived."

Knowing how often she had accused him of being

a Brigand and a robber, she could not meet his eyes.

Next they were meeting the Members of Parliament who had been listening to what had been said through the open doors behind them.

Once again it struck Ileana how old most of them looked and she was quite certain it did not escape the notice of the man beside her.

Another surprise, which she knew was part of Prince Vladilas's plan, was that they were to have luncheon with the Prime Minister and the Cabinet.

"I must apologise," the Prime Minister said, "if the luncheon is not as elaborate as might have been demanded by such circumstances, but we did not have very long to arrange it."

Then in a different tone he said to Ileana:

"I cannot tell Your Royal Highness how thrilled I am that, after your refusal to entertain our plea that you should be married, you should have chosen a husband who is Zokālan, and who belongs to us as we belong to him!"

Ileana was tempted to retort that he had chosen her and she had had no choice in the matter, but she knew it was something she must not say.

She merely replied by looking down and smiling, hoping the Prime Minister would think she was too shy to talk about it.

Prince Vladilas however was entirely at his ease.

He made everybody laugh at luncheon as he recounted anecdotes about his father and mother.

He also told them that a number of his men were the sons, and even the grandsons of men who had followed his father when he left the country, 'shaking,' as Prince Alexander had vowed, 'the dust of Zokāla off my feet for ever.'

Then more seriously Prince Vladilas went on to say:

"I visited my family Castle six months ago, and I realised then that you have neglected the Mispa Valley in which it stands in the same way that you have neglected Bela."

There was, Ileana thought, a slightly embarrassed look on the faces of some of the Ministers at the table, but the Prince continued:

"From what my father told me, and from my own observations I am certain that the Mispa Valley has tremendous potential."

"I have never been there," the Prime Minister said, "but I always understood it was barren and desolated."

"It is at the moment," Prince Vladilas agreed, "but there is a great deal of game in the high mountains which form a defensive barrier against Rumania. There is plenty of water in the valley which could easily be cultivated, and my father told me there are precious stones and marble in the mountains which have never been mined."

He looked at the men listening to him for a moment before he said:

"I shall settle a great many of my followers there. They will build houses and set up new crafts, and I am quite certain, knowing how talented and industrious they are, that they will soon be in competition with the people in this valley, which will prove an incentive to the whole country."

He paused before he went on:

"The trained soldiers I have with me can teach the younger members of the Zokālan Army how to use our new weapons, and there are a great many more to come."

"More?" the Minister for Defence ejaculated. "If it is not an impertinent question, Your Royal Highness, may I ask how all these guns and weapons are to be paid for?"

"That is a sensible question, and one that must obviously be answered," the Prince replied. "For the time being let them be my gift to my country to which I am so happily restored. In the many years during which my father was in exile he accumulated a very large fortune."

He glanced at Ileana and she saw that his eyes were twinkling as he went on:

"I think even my wife believes that Bandits and robbers live only by thieving from other people. That may sometimes be true, but what we have done on our travels over the Balkans is to thieve ideas, and to envisage lucrative possibilities which have never entered the heads of the Statesmen of the country in question."

He gave a short laugh before he went on:

"I think you will find that the new type of rifle which my Army is using and which can be quite easily made in our own Factories, once we have built them, will within a year, be in great demand from almost every other country in Europe."

Ileana thought the Minister of Defence looked a

little sceptical, but Prince Vladilas continued:

"We have also perfected a means of transporting weapons and other military equipment across rivers and mountains that is almost foolproof, while at the same time difficult to imitate except by buying the secret of its manufacture from us."

He threw out his hands in an expressive gesture as he said:

"We have dozens of ideas, some of which we admit to having stolen, some of which have merely evolved through necessity. They will certainly now that we are settling down, add very considerably to the prosperity of Zokāla."

There was no need to look at the expression on the faces of the men listening to realise they were tremendously impressed by all the Prince had said.

In spite of the welcome he had received, when the luncheon ended Ileana realised that he was impatient to leave.

He managed to stave off the questions that were being put to him, and which succeeded each other so quickly that Ileana thought it would be impossible for them ever to get away.

And yet by some magic of his own Prince Vladilas brought the luncheon to a close and they moved to where the carriage was waiting outside in the Market Place.

When they had said goodbye to the Prime Minister and were driving towards the Palace, Ileana thought it was characteristic that the good wishes of the populace could only be expressed in flowers.

It seemed as if everybody waiting in the Market Place had flowers in their hands.

They threw them into the carriage as it moved slowly towards the gold-tipped gates which led into the garden surrounding the beautiful building that had been erected on a natural hill overlooking the City two centuries earlier.

The building outside was as beautiful and as romantic as the interior.

The domes and spires which were embellished with gold seemed to reflect the sunlight and Ileana thought, although he did not say anything, that Prince Vladilas looked at them appreciatively.

At last they drew up outside the impressive porticoed entrance where the Palace servants in their white and gold livery were waiting for them, as were the Counsellors of State and the Gentlemen-in-Waiting.

Again there were congratulations and Ileana realised they accepted Prince Vladilas with an enthusiasm they would not have accorded to any foreign Prince.

Then at last they were alone in the beautiful Drawing-Room opening into the garden where her mother had always sat, and which was known as 'The Queen's Room.'

It was then that Ileana felt she must ask again the question she had asked immediately after her husband had introduced himself to their people.

"Why did you not tell me? Why did you think it was clever to deceive me?"

"I did not deceive you," Prince Vladilas replied. "You merely assumed that I was what I appeared to be, and there was nothing wrong in that. I have been a Brigand and a robber and, as I have already explained, at times rather a special kind of thief. And yet it is a life which I think has given me an insight into the problems which await me here."

"And when you have solved them all you will obviously be very bored," Ileana exclaimed.

He shrugged his shoulders.

"Perhaps! That is a risk I have to take, but I suppose every man has to settle down sometime in his life."

There was a twist to his lips which made Ileana think he was being sarcastic and she said:

"I suppose if you find it intolerable you can always go back to your mountains."

"Are you trying to tempt me into doing so already?" Prince Vladilas asked in an amused voice. "I think I might first find out how my men acclimatise themselves to Zokāla, and of course, my horses."

Because she could not help it Ileana's eyes brightened as she thought of the Arab mares and stallions she had seen across the river last night.

Impulsively she cried:

"You know I want to ride your Arab horses! When may I do so?"

"Tomorrow, if you wish," Prince Vladilas replied. "I suppose you have a respectable habit to wear in which to ride?"

If he had meant to be deliberately provocative, he certainly succeeded.

Ileana flushed and her eyes glinted at him as she said:

"I will not be dictated to as to what I should or should not wear! It is impossible to school an unbroken horse while I am wearing a skirt!"

"Then I will school them for you," Prince Vladilas said calmly. "Let me make this quite clear, Ileana: You will never again, as long as you are my wife, wear trousers!"

"In which case," Ileana retorted, "the sooner you go back to the mountains, the better! Or perhaps I can dispose of you in some other way!"

She spoke impulsively, then wondered if she had gone too far.

Instead the Prince merely threw back his head and laughed.

"I thought we would not go far before once again I had to impress upon you the fact that I always get my own way! If I find you disobeying my rules, then you will undoubtedly regret it!"

"Are you still contemplating beating me?" Ileana asked provocatively, "and is it to be a private or a public flogging?"

"That all depends," the Prince replied. "It would certainly prove a salutory lesson to other offenders if the wife of their Ruler was seen to be punished in the Market Place!"

She was sure he was speaking jokingly, and yet she had the uncomfortable feeling that he would not hesitate to punish her if she really offended against what he called his 'Rules.'

Then she gave a little stamp of her foot as she said:

"You are getting everything your own way, are you

not? You have got my people eating out of your hand, and all those stupid old Politicians think you are saving their faces and that their inefficiency will be covered up and forgotten."

"I am delighted to know you recognise how inefficient they are," Prince Vladilas said. "It is criminal the way they have allowed the country to sink into a complacency that has risked, if not the lives, at least the independence of every Zokālan."

He spoke scathingly, and then as Ileana did not reply he said:

"You yourself must bear a great deal of the blame. You have imagination and an unusual amount of intelligence for a woman, but you could not see what was staring you in the face: that Hungary, Rumania or Serbia could gobble you up and hardly lose one soldier in the process."

Because she knew he was right it made Ileana all the more angry.

"That is your story, and you have made everybody believe it," she said, "but personally, I think you have invented it to suit your own ends. I have always found our neighbours to be charming and full of goodwill towards us and as I have had proposals of marriage from the Royal Families of most of them, I just do not believe your bogey-bogey story, which you have thought up to frighten us."

"Now you are being childish!" Prince Vladilas said. "I am not going to argue with you any further because you are only trying to excuse what is inexcusable."

"I can see you are very pleased with yourself,"

Ileana remarked, "and so I concede there is nothing to be gained by arguing. But quite frankly I do not believe that we need saving as you so volubly insist. Of course your theory has been an excellent step up into the place you wanted for yourself!"

"Of course," the Prince agreed mildly, "and who could put it more delicately and with more diplomacy than you, my dear?"

The way he spoke annoyed Ileana more than ever.

"What you are trying to do," she said, "is to turn this country into an arsenal of weapons of destruction. We are very happy as we are and always have been, tending our crops with which we can feed ourselves, practising a large number of crafts which have kept the women busy, and breeding, however clever you may think you have been with your Arab strain, the best horses in the whole of Europe!"

"Horses! Of course that is the operative word!" the Prince exclaimed. "Horses have obsessed you until you can see nothing else. How long does a horse last in a modern battle where gunshot brings them to their knees, however fast they can gallop?"

His voice was serious as he went on:

"If you had ever seen the suffering of the horses in the battlefield, as I have, you would know that sooner or later somebody has to invent a vehicle which will take the place of horses, and which will not scream in agony when it is hit by bullets, or the rider is blown up by explosive shells from a gun."

He spoke so intensely that Ileana looked at him in astonishment.

"What are you saying?" she asked.

"I believe that in the future, though it may be a long way ahead," he replied, "human beings, when they wish to kill each other, will do so without involving animals who do not understand."

Because there was a note in his voice when he spoke of the suffering of the horses which Ileana had never heard before, she felt her anger slipping away.

No man could be wholly bad who loved horses to the point where he could speak of their being wounded or killed in a manner which told her how much he suffered with them.

Impulsively she moved closer to him as she said:

"I am sure you are right, though it sounds as though it must be impossible. But it is something with which I would like to help you."

He looked at her, and the frown that had been between his eyes vanished.

"Why not?" he asked. "Perhaps together we can invent something sensational."

"I would like that."

"For the moment," the Prince said, "my horses are there for you to tell me if they are as good as or better than yours."

"I shall never admit that," Ileana replied, "and I will match *Satan* against any horse you produce."

She realised that Prince Vladilas raised his eyebrows as she explained:

"*Satan* is my stallion, and I think it would be impossible for anybody to find a faster horse."

"That is certainly a challenge," the Prince said quietly, "in addition to all the other challenges you offer me."

She wondered what he meant by that, but did not like to ask him.

She looked up at him and Ileana saw that his eyes were on her unbound hair.

Again impulsively, as if she could not help it, she asked:

"Are you comparing me to your Greek women? I know by the way you spoke of your mother that you thought they could not be equalled by the women of any other country."

"That is true," the Prince replied, "with one exception."

Because of the way he spoke, which was a little dryly, Ileana asked quite ingenuously:

"Which is that?"

"Yours!"

She looked at him in astonishment. Then she asked:

"Are you really paying me a compliment?"

"I think actually, I am stating a fact," he replied. "You are very beautiful, Ileana, as you must be aware, but in a different way from the Greek women who are dark and, like my mother, most of them are very soft, sweet and feminine."

Ileana stiffened.

He was speaking the very words that described the Greek girl who had looked after her last night and who she was sure meant something very special to him.

"I am sorry if I disappoint you," she said lightly, "but of course, as you married me to make sure of the throne of Zokāla, you really had no choice. I might almost say I was a 'pig in a poke!'"

"That is not quite true," the Prince replied, "but we are married, Ileana, and I think we ought to be intelligent about it."

"I am interested to know what you mean by that."

"Shall I explain?"

As he spoke she found herself thinking of how last night when she had threatened him with the knife he had flung her back on the bed and fallen on top of her.

She felt almost as if she could feel again the weight of his body, the ease with which he had rendered her completely helpless, and the pain in her wrist when he had forced her to drop the knife onto the floor.

Because the memory of it perturbed her, her eyes dropped before his, and she looked away from him to say sharply:

"You have explained very eloquently who you are, but that does not change my feelings towards you. As I told you last night, I hate you! I will play the part of your wife in public, because it is for the good of my countrymen, but if you come near me when we are alone, I swear I will find some way of killing you!"

There was a little pause as her voice seemed to vibrate in the beautiful room.

Then Prince Vladilas said again with that dry note in his voice:

"Now we know exactly where we stand!"

"Exactly!" Ileana agreed. "So be careful! Another time I shall not be so foolish as to be caught by the trick you played on me last night!"

"It is most gracious of you to warn me," he replied.

She gave a little stamp of her foot and walked away from him, and at that moment the door opened.

"The Prime Minister, Your Royal Highness," the Butler's voice announced, "the Lord Chamberlain, and His Grace the Archbishop."

To Ileana's surprise the three men came slowly into the room.

As the door closed quietly behind them the Prime Minister said to Ileana:

"It is my sad and very painful duty to inform Your Royal Highness that His Majesty King Milko is dead!"

"Dead!" Ileana repeated.

She had been meaning ever since arriving back at the Palace to go up to her father's room, but she had been beguiled into arguing, or rather fighting with Prince Vladilas.

Anyway, she had not expected there to be any recovery from the coma in which her father had lain unconscious for the last five months.

Now she clasped her fingers together, knowing that to hear that he was actually no longer breathing was a shock, even though it had been inevitable for so long.

She was aware that the Prince had moved to stand beside her.

Then the Prime Minister said in a different tone of voice:

"The King is dead! Long live the King and Queen!"

As he spoke he went down on one knee before them.

chapter six

THE Funeral was over and Ileana had to admire the way in which it had been arranged.

To cope with the arrival of the distinguished visitors and innumerable relatives everything had been perfectly organised by Vladilas.

She could see his hand in everything: in the Funeral Cortège which was extremely impressive, and the manner in which in order of precedence the Kings and Princes from other countries were received and accommodated.

Every relative, no matter whether he was important or unimportant, was welcomed and looked after.

She knew, although she disliked admitting it, that she would have found it a very difficult task to carry out herself, and undoubtedly the Prime Minister and other Members of the Cabinet would have made a mess of it.

The only people who were at all discomfited were the elderly Generals who found themselves being given orders instead of giving them and were inevitably very envious of the new weapons and the strange-looking soldiers who manned them.

There was an enormous number of people to be catered for in the Palace, but by a miracle the Chefs, obviously having a great deal of extra help, managed it.

Although it was an undoubtedly gloomy occasion, there was at the dinner-table laughter besides a lot of intelligent conversation.

Sitting at the other end of the large table from Vladilas, who had taken the place her father used to occupy, Ileana, even while she told herself she hated him, had to admit he made a very handsome and resplendent King.

Dressed in the uniform of the Commander-in-Chief of the Zokālan Army, he made a brilliant patch of colour among the sombre black of the mourners.

Ileana on the other hand, hated the dark veil that she had to wear over her face and her gown, which she thought made her look like a raven.

Actually it was a perfect frame for the translucence of her skin, and accentuated the red-gold of her hair.

What was more, the green of her eyes seemed to gleam like emeralds, and more than one Prince from the neighbouring countries looked at her reproachfully because she had refused his offer of marriage.

She was in The Queen's Room alone the day after the Funeral, having already said goodbye to a number of relatives and Crowned Heads, when the door opened and Prince Tomilav came in.

She smiled and put out her hand saying:

"I am so glad you were sent to represent your country, and not some disagreeable Minister like the one from Hungary!"

Prince Tomilav knew she was referring to the Hungarian who had made it obvious that his interest was not in mourning King Milko, but in inspecting the guns and new weapons of war which Vladilas had put very prominently on display.

The gun-carriage which had carried the King's coffin to the Cathedral was different from any other gun-carriage to be seen in the Northern part of the Balkans.

To make certain that their readiness for war was apparent there was a display of troops and their weapons on the Parade Ground.

"You know as well as I do," Prince Tomilav said as he joined Ileana in the window, "that my country would never go to war with yours any more than I would fight you!"

That was true, Ileana knew, and because she realised from the way he had looked at her yesterday and last night that he was still very much in love she said:

"I hope, Tomilav, you will always be my friend."

"I have no wish to be your friend," he replied. "I love you, Ileana, as I shall never love anybody else. If only you had accepted me, I know we would have been very happy."

Ileana gave a little sigh.

She was wondering whether in fact, she would rather have married Tomilav than the Brigand who had forced her into marriage without her having a chance of refusing him.

Because she felt that in some way she was scoring over Vladilas by being nice to Tomilav she said softly:

"It is too late now, and there is nothing we can do . . . about it."

She saw the light come into his eyes from the way she spoke, and he put out his hand to take hers saying:

"I love you! I love you until I cannot sleep for thinking about you, and when I heard that you were married, I wanted to shoot myself!"

"No! No!" Ileana exclaimed, "you must not talk like that. I married Vladilas in order to save Zokāla since we were in danger of being overrun by Hungary. The sight of all these weapons will certainly deter them."

"You do not love him?" Prince Tomilav asked in a low voice. "You swear that is true?"

"I hate him!" Ileana answered. "But now he is my husband and the King, and there is no escape."

"My darling, if only I could take you away and make you happy."

He kissed her hand passionately with hot, burning kisses.

Then as she looked at him with a warmth in her eyes she had never shown him before, he said:

"If you ever want me, you know I will come to you—from the ends of the earth, if necessary! You fill my life, Ileana, and it will be impossible for me ever to love anybody else."

"You must not think like that," Ileana said quickly. "You must try to forget me."

"Never!"

She sighed.

"I shall never forget that you are my friend."

She spoke softly and, encouraged as he had never been in the past, Prince Tomilav reached out to put his hands on her shoulders.

"Before I go, Ileana," he said in a hoarse voice, "and it is doubtful if I shall ever come back, let me kiss you."

Ileana hesitated, then she asked herself why should she care if it was disloyal to a man who had no real interest in her except that she was a stepping-stone to power.

As if her hesitation made him think she consented, Prince Tomilav pulled her close against him, but when his lips sought hers she turned her head so that they rested against her cheek.

"I love you! Oh, darling, I love you!" he murmured hoarsely.

At that moment the door opened.

Neither of them realised that Vladilas was in the room until he walked towards them, and as he reached them Prince Tomilav took his arms from around Ileana and stepped back.

Then as she looked at her husband she knew she had never seen a man look so furiously angry or so frightening.

She thought he resembled an eagle or some other great bird of prey, and there was an expression that seemed like murder in his eyes.

"Get out of here!" he said to Prince Tomilav. "And if you are still in the Palace in fifteen minute's time, I swear I will kill you!"

The vehemence of his words seemed to vibrate around the room, and Prince Tomilav went very pale before with an effort to appear dignified he walked towards the door and turning the handle left the room.

Vladilas stood watching him go and only when the door closed did he turn towards Ileana.

Although she tried to face him defiantly, she felt her heart beating tumultuously because he looked so terrifying.

"How dare you!" he said furiously. "How dare you allow another man to touch you when you are my wife!"

Ileana lifted her chin.

"A wife chosen to further your ambitions!" she retorted. "And you have no right to interfere with my friends."

"Friends? Do you call that friendship?" Vladilas asked scornfully.

Then as he looked at her, the flames of red glinting in her hair, her green eyes defying him, he lost his self-control.

Taking her by the shoulders as Prince Tomilav had done, but with his fingers digging violently into the softness of her flesh, he shook her.

He shook her as if she was a small animal, backwards and forwards until the pins flew out of her hair, her chignon loosened and the heavy tresses fell down her back.

Still he shook her until she was breathless.

Then as she put up her hands to try to force him away from her he pulled her violently against him and said furiously:

"If it is kisses you want, why not take them from the man who is entitled to kiss you!"

With that his lips were on hers, and Ileana wanted to cry out with the pain of it.

He kissed her roughly, brutally, and while she wanted to plead with him not to hurt her she was captive and helpless in his arms which were like bands of steel.

Then as if the softness and inexperience of her lips swept away some of the anger, Vladilas's mouth became more gentle though no less insistent.

Now his kisses were demanding, dominating, but at the same time there was a tenderness that had not been there before, and the pain he had caused her ceased.

Ileana had never been kissed, and she had not realised that a woman could be held completely captive in a man's arms in a way which made it impossible not only to move, but even to think.

Then, as she wanted to struggle against him and free her lips from his, she found his mouth had evoked a strange sensation within her which was something quite different from anything she had ever felt in the past.

She could not explain it, it was almost as if a tidal wave swept over her and she was no longer herself, but a part of Vladilas.

Then when it seemed that every conflicting feeling in her whole body was concentrated in her breasts, he suddenly took his arms from her.

She would have fallen to the ground if she had not reached out to hold onto the back of a chair.

Without speaking, without even looking at her, he

walked out of the room, slamming the door behind him, and Ileana heard his footsteps going down the corridor.

It was then she felt as if she had been engulfed in a tempestuous sea and had been so buffeted by it that she could hardly believe she was still alive and not drowned.

Trembling, because it had all been so unexpected and such a shock, she sat down in a chair and covered her face with her hands.

She could feel the pain of Vladilas's fingers still on her shoulders, and she thought her lips must be bruised because of the way he had first kissed her.

And yet there was still that strange feeling within her which seemed, now she could think about it, to intensify and to burn through her whole body so that she could not escape from it.

"How dare he treat me in such a way?" she tried to say.

But there was no real anger behind the words and they were in fact as ineffective and helpless as she was herself.

As she heard the door open, she hastily sat up in her chair and put up her hands to tidy her hair.

"Excuse me, Your Majesty," one of the *Aides-de-Camp* said from the doorway, "but His Majesty King Otto of Greece wishes to say goodbye to Your Majesty before he leaves."

"Tell His Majesty I will be with him in a few minutes," Ileana replied.

The *Aide-de-Camp* bowed and shut the door, and she quickly picked up her hairpins from where they had fallen on the floor.

Whatever her private life was like at the moment, she must publicly behave as was expected of a Queen, with gracious dignity.

As she walked along the corridor to the State Room where she knew the King, and doubtless other departing dignitaries would be waiting, she recalled that in the past she had often thought that the Kings and Queens with whom she had stayed were so frigid and formal that it was impossible for them to feel any normal human emotion.

Now she told herself her whole body was a battle-ground of feelings that she could not translate into words.

She only knew they left her confused, agitated, and conscious that her heart was beating in a very strange manner.

"How could he do this to me?" she asked herself, and thought with a feeling almost of despair that the future with Vladilas as her husband was very frightening.

* * *

By the following morning the last visitor had left and the Palace seemed extremely quiet.

It was not only the Crowned Heads or their representatives from nearly a dozen countries who had occupied all the best bedrooms, it was that they had each brought with them a retinue.

There were Equerries, secretaries, valets, medical attendants, Gentlemen-in-Waiting and, in the case of one Monarch, besides his doctor there was a chiropodist.

Ileana could not help thinking that if Vladilas had had been a husband she had chosen for herself they would have been able to laugh in private at their guests.

They would wonder how many of them, when they saw the parade of arms which the Zokālan Army now possessed, would realise that their ambitions were defeated without a single shot being fired.

Instead, after what had occurred, she was aware that Vladilas would not speak to her: He did not look at her and was obviously going out of his way to avoid her.

The only time he was even near her was when it was time for them to retire.

Then they said good night to their guests and left the State Drawing-Room formally with Ileana's hand resting on the King's.

In the Hall he walked with her to the bottom of the staircase, bowed and left her without speaking as she started to ascend the stairs.

She was sure he was still very angry, and as she walked towards her own bedroom she wondered how long they could continue to ignore each other.

She felt it was, in fact, very much more depressing than if they were fighting.

Ileana admitted that she would rather enjoy a duel in words, in which she would try if not to hurt Vladilas, because she was sure that was impossible, at least to provoke him.

All she could see now were long, frustrating days ahead when, if he wished, he could arrange everything without even consulting her.

It would be exactly what the Prime Minister and the Cabinet would think correct.

They had always resented that a woman should give them orders, and she was quite certain they would not wish her to attend their meetings or, if they could prevent it, to have any part in the governing of Zokāla.

"I will fight him! I will fight him on this, if nothing else!" Ileana cried.

Then she remembered how helpless she had felt in his arms and how strong he had been and hated herself for being a woman rather than a man.

"I would be the King now if I had been a boy!" she kept saying.

She wanted to defy Vladilas by wearing the trousers in which she had schooled her horses and which had given her a sense of freedom, but which, if she obeyed him, she would never wear again.

She lay awake for a long time, tossing and turning and wondering how she could bear a life in which she was forced into having nothing to do except to sit about the Palace and play at being a Queen.

She felt heavy-eyed in the morning, and rose almost as soon as she was called.

Putting on again the black gown, but resentfully because it seemed so inappropriate on such a sunny day, she went downstairs to The Queen's Room, wondering what Vladilas was doing.

There were a number of letters on her writing-table.

They were all condolences which she knew she had to answer, but she pushed them aside, conscious that no more State Papers such as those which had been brought to her after her father had become ill and which she had signed on his behalf, were there.

Vladilas would have those now, and doubtless he was putting all sorts of plans into operation, considering new Acts of Parliament, and enjoying the respect of the Ministers who would listen to him without daring to express their own opinions.

As if fresh anger was engendered by her thoughts, she swept away the pile of letters of condolence from her desk to the floor.

She thought as she did so that they were typical trivialities which would be all that was left to her from now until she was in the grave.

Then as she stood looking down at the letters that were strewn at her feet, and instead of feeling angry, curiously near to tears, the door opened and Vladilas came into the room.

Almost despite herself, Ileana felt her heart leap just because he was there.

He was not in uniform, but wearing riding-clothes and looking extremely handsome.

"I came to tell you that I am leaving this morning for Mispa," he said in a cold, distant voice that made him sound as if he was speaking to her from several miles away.

Ileana's eyes widened as he went on:

"I am taking with me a large number of my followers whom I intend to settle there, and as it will take sometime to make all the arrangements for their comfort, I expect to be away for perhaps ten days or two weeks."

He paused but still Ileana found it impossible to say anything, and he went on:

"Any documents of importance will of course be brought to me every day, and I expect you will be able to deal with any other matters."

He finished speaking and as if he expected no reply he turned to leave the room.

Only as he reached the door did Ileana find her voice and without thinking the words came out a little jerkily:

"Let me ... come with ... you."

Vladilas already had the door half-open and now he paused and still with his back to her he asked:

"Is that what you want?"

Impulsively Ileana moved towards him, and as he turned round she said:

"Please ... please ... let me come with you."

His eyes searched her face as if he was asking if what he had heard was the truth.

Then as she looked up at him pleadingly he said:

"I will order your horse *Satan* and we will leave in an hour."

He was gone before she could reply.

Then because she had a frightening feeling that if she was late he would not wait for her, she ran as quickly as she could up to her bedroom.

*   *   *

Riding through the valley it was very hot, and as Ileana looked up at the last small vestige of snow on the mountain peaks she felt that just the sight of them helped to cool her.

Since she had not been able to ride *Satan* during the days of the Funeral, he was very fresh and obstreperous, and she was certain that because the grooms were frightened of him he had not been properly exercised.

He bucked and reared as soon as she was in the saddle, just to show his independence, and she had the feeling that Vladilas was watching her control him with a twinkle in his eyes.

She was determined to prove to him that not only was *Satan* an exceptional horse, but she was an exceptional rider.

It was with a feeling of satisfaction, which was as warm as the sunshine, that as they rode on she knew by an instinct stronger than words that Vladilas was no longer angry with her.

She had been determined to look her best and had swept aside her lady's-maid's suggestion that she should wear a black habit.

Instead, knowing that everybody would be horrified if she wore one of her coloured ones, she chose one of white piqué that was smart yet cool on the hottest day.

It had a riding-hat with a white gauze veil encircling the crown and hanging down her back.

She knew because of what lay ahead that her eyes were sparkling, and she looked her best as she came down the steps of the Palace to where Vladilas was waiting for her.

To her surprise, instead of allowing one of the grooms to assist her, he himself lifted her into the saddle.

As he arranged her full riding-skirt over her stirrup she thought there was a faint twist to his lips, as if he knew he had been the victor in his determination that she should not ride in trousers.

He certainly could not accuse her of being anything but feminine, she thought, in her white riding-habit with a thin muslin blouse beneath it and a bunch of lace at her throat.

Her gloves were white and her whip had an ivory handle set with small diamonds.

She thought he looked at her appreciatively, but could not be sure.

When he had mounted his own horse, a magnificent Arab-bred animal with an arched neck that would have proclaimed his origin anywhere, they set off at the head of a cavalcade that Ileana thought might have stepped out of a story-book.

As they reached the valley she looked back and saw that with his characteristically inimitable and efficient organisation, Vladilas must have commandeered every possible vehicle not only from the Army, but from the civilian population in order to convey his people to the valley.

He was taking there, she thought, all the women and children she had first seen with him, but now there seemed to be many more of them than there had been before.

The vehicles were piled high with their possessions, and walking behind them led on ropes were not only their horses but their cows and goats.

She looked back and saw in the rear of the cavalcade there were many drays stacked with wood, posts, and what she suspected were a large number of building implements.

Then she said to Vladilas:

"Anybody seeing us would be quite certain we were the Israelites, setting out for the Promised land!"

"That is what I believe the Mispa Valley will be to my people," Vladilas replied, "and once they have homes they will settle down and be happy."

"What happened to the homes they originally had?" Ileana enquired.

There was a little pause and she had the feeling he was wondering if he should be truthful or not. Then he said:

"Some of them are the descendants of those who followed my father when he left Zokāla. Some, as I suspect you have already guessed, have their own reasons for leaving their countries of origin, and some are in hiding."

"Do you mean they are criminals?"

"I mean they came to me for protection," he said in a cold voice, "and that is something I would refuse nobody!"

There was silence until Ileana asked:

"And you think they will be happy, now that you are looking after them?"

"That is what I intend them to be," Vladilas replied. "So we must both make every effort to make them feel that they are actually an important part of our country."

It flashed through her mind that she was surprised that he included her, then because *Satan* was being restless she asked:

"Can we give the horses their heads? Or will our people feel we have deserted them?"

Vladilas gave a little laugh.

"As most of them are experienced horsemen," he said, "I think they will understand what we are doing."

Ileana smiled, and touching *Satan* with her whip set off at a wild gallop.

She knew it was a challenge which Vladilas would not refuse, and in a moment they were racing over the flower-filled grass, hearing the thunder of hoofs, and feeling the cool air sweep away the heat and dust of the city.

It was so exhilarating that when a long time later Ileana drew in *Satan* she felt as if she had suddenly come alive and the depression she had been feeling for the last twenty-four hours had been swept away.

"Did I win?" she asked, knowing it was only a question in any case of a few inches.

"It was a dead heat!" Vladilas said firmly. "We

were equal, which is as it should be."

She knew there was an innuendo in his voice and he was not only speaking of the race.

"That is what I hoped you might say," she answered.

She looked at him as she spoke. But he was turning his horse back towards the procession behind them, and as he was already moving quickly she had to hurry to catch up with him.

It was only when they reached the Mispa Valley and Vladilas was giving directions as to where everybody was to go, that she was able to look more closely at the people who had been behind them.

It was then she saw Thelia.

She was looking very lovely sitting at the front of a wagon that was packed with other women and a number of their children.

She was wearing a large-brimmed hat to protect her beautiful face from the sun, and the ribbons that tied under her chin which were of rose pink accentuated the dark of her hair and the perfection of her skin.

She did not see Ileana looking at her, for her eyes were on Vladilas giving directions, and she was looking at him yearningly and with love.

Ileana turned away abruptly and a few minutes later they were riding towards the Castle.

Set almost at the end of the valley with thick woods which covered the lower part of the mountain behind them, it was exactly, Ileana thought, as a Castle should look.

It reminded her vaguely of the Castles she had seen

in Bavaria, and had a number of small turrets pointing up to the sky.

From the distance it had a fairy-tale appearance that gave it a look of enchantment.

"I am afraid you must expect to rough it a little," Vladilas said as they drew nearer the Castle, "because although I sent some of my people to the Castle as soon as I reached Zokāla so that it could be opened up, it has been empty for a long time, and the caretakers in charge have grown very old."

"Do you mean that nobody has lived there since your father left?"

He shook his head.

"No, it was just waiting, I feel, for me to come home."

The way he spoke was rather moving, and Ileana hoped for his sake that he would not be disappointed.

She found however when she entered the Castle that it was furnished very attractively, and somebody, she was sure on Vladilas's instructions, had put flowers in every room.

They helped to conceal the fact that the curtains and carpets were faded, and many of the chairs needed recovering.

But if it had seemed like a fairy-tale Palace from a distance, near to it had a charm that was very different from the romantic beauty of her own Palace.

There were portraits on the walls of Vladilas's ancestors.

Although the furniture needed polishing, it was the

product of skilled craftsmen who she knew in the past had worked there.

She felt sure that if one looked for them now they could still be found working at their trade in the small villages in the mountains.

She wandered from room to room without Vladilas because he was still organising his people and supervising the raising of tents in which they must live and sleep until their cottages were built.

From the Castle windows Ileana could see that the land down by the river which ran through the centre of the valley was rich and verdant.

There was a huge lake below the Castle which reflected not only the sky but also the peaks of the mountains towering just behind them.

'I could be very happy here,' she thought involuntarily.

Then it was almost as if somebody asked:

"With Vladilas?"

He was away for a long time, but an hour later her luggage, which her lady's-maid from the Palace had packed hastily, arrived in a brake drawn by six horses.

With it came one of her younger lady's-maids because Ileana had thought it would be a mistake to bring any of the older ones who were very set in their ways and disliked change of any sort.

Greta was a bright, rosy-cheeked young girl, only just beginning to learn how to look after Ileana's gowns and eager to do everything right.

Ileana liked her, but she chattered in a manner which the older maids disapproved of.

"It's lovely here, Your Majesty!" Greta exclaimed. "I couldn't believe it when I was told I was to come with Your Majesty and look after you."

"I am sure you will manage very well, Greta," Ileana replied, "and now I would like to have a bath and change."

Greta hurried off to arrange it, and when she had gone Ileana looked around her bedroom which she knew had last been used by Vladilas's grandmother.

His father had not been married until after he was exiled, and his Greek wife had therefore never seen the Castle which had been so close to her husband's heart.

As Ileana remembered she was Greek, she thought of Thelia coming to the valley and wondered if it had been a disappointment to her and perhaps also to Vladilas when she had joined the expedition.

"Perhaps they wanted to be together," she told herself, and was surprised that she felt not angry, but upset at the idea.

It was then she asked herself why Vladilas had planned to leave without preparing her for his departure, and had merely informed her that he was going in an hour's time and would not be back for at least ten days.

Had he wanted to spend those ten days with Thelia? Was that where his real interest lay?

She could remember all too clearly Thelia's soft voice saying to her:

"Please be...kind to him. He is...so very... wonderful!"

She had heard the throb on the words and was sure she had tears in her eyes as she said them.

She loved him, and of course he loved her because his mother was Greek.

Suddenly Ileana could not understand why the thought of their loving each other made her feel lost and somehow afraid.

"Of course there have been women, doubtless dozens of them, in Vladilas's life," she told herself.

He was handsome, a man, and if the Zokālans were famous for being ardent lovers, so were the Greeks.

It would have been impossible for him with both Zokālan and Greek blood in his veins to live a life of chastity.

And why should he?

He was a Brigand and took what he wanted, and the Pallikares were famous for stealing not only a man's possessions, if they needed them, but also his women-folk, if they desired them.

She tried not to think of the way Vladilas had kissed her, and the manner in which his lips had first hurt her, then evoked strange sensations which she could still feel flickering through her when she thought about them.

"He was just punishing me!" she told herself.

The whole incident was so disturbing that she tried to put it out of her mind, but found it impossible.

Greta came back to say that her bath was ready and she found leading out of her bedroom there was a small octagonal bathroom which she was sure was enclosed by one of the turrets.

She knew now that her own room had a dome overhead that had glinted gold in the sunshine as they had ridden towards it.

"It is a Fairy Castle," she told herself.

She tried not to think that Vladilas, as far as she was concerned, was not playing the part of Prince Charming, but of an Ogre who, if he did not terrorise the countryside, certainly managed to terrorise her.

When she finished her bath she put on a pretty summer gown that was more simple than those she wore in the Palace.

"I expect, Your Majesty, you are hungry," Greta said. "It is long after midday."

Ileana had completely forgotten that if she had been at home she would have had luncheon by now.

Then she remembered that Vladilas had said he was used to eating two meals a day—breakfast and dinner.

At the Funeral he had certainly appeared at luncheontime to play host to their relations and distinguished guests, but she had the idea that today he would be too preoccupied.

She was right. When she reached the Hall an *Aide-de-Camp* came hurrying through the door. When he saw her he pulled himself to attention and clicked his heels.

"A message from His Majesty, Ma'am!"

"What is it, Captain Heviz?" Ileana asked.

"His Majesty deeply regrets that as he is so busily engaged he cannot join Your Majesty for luncheon and hopes you will excuse him. He will come to the Castle as soon as he is free."

Ileana smiled.

"I am sure His Majesty is very busy!"

The formal expression on the *Aide-de-Camp's* face changed to a boyish grin.

"He is working harder than anybody, Ma'am," he said. "There is nobody like His Majesty! He is marvellous!"

There was so much enthusiasm in the young man's voice that Ileana gave a little laugh.

"I am glad it is all working out to plan," she said and walked away towards the Dining-Room.

It was a simple meal but well-cooked, and she was sure that Vladilas's magic touch had already reached the kitchens.

As soon as she had finished she started to explore the Castle and to her surprise found herself wishing that Vladilas was there to explain some of the pictures to her.

There were also many objects which she supposed were family treasures that amazingly had not been stolen since his father left the country.

Then because after the long ride she had to admit she was tired, she went to her rooms and thought she might rest.

Instead she explored her suite in the Castle and found that out of her bedroom which was very impressive with the silk bed-curtains hanging from a gold corona with rioting gold cupids, there led a Sitting-Room.

Ileana realised that the exquisitely painted carvings on the frames and round the mirrors which was the work of the native craftsmen had made every room seem very colourful.

In the Sitting-Room were rugs of white fur beside those woven by the women from the villages with brilliant coloured patterns.

There was also exquisitely inlaid furniture and pictures that must have been handed down for generations.

There were huge vases filled with flowers in every room which scented the air and took away what she thought with the opening of the Castle must have been the mustiness of age.

She opened the door leading from the other side of the Sitting-Room to find what she was certain was Vladilas's bedroom.

There was no mistaking the huge, four-poster bed, carved and decorated with the same colours as her own bedroom, but hung with dark red velvet curtains and with the Royal Coat-of-Arms embellished with his father's crest over the bedhead.

It was a man's room, but had the charm which was to be found in every room in the house.

Again there were flowers that made it seem very lived-in and it was difficult to believe that nobody had slept there for over thirty years.

As she felt it was almost too intimate to be in her husband's room, Ileana quickly went back into her own and lay down on the bed.

She only meant to rest for a short time, but when she awoke the sun had sunk behind the mountains and she was aware that down in the valley below there were lights which came from the fires outside the tents.

The people they had brought with them would be cooking their evening meal, and she thought she could hear the sound of violins in the distance and was sure that the Gypsies were there.

She had a sudden wish to join them to listen to the Gypsy music and watch the dancing.

She had the frightening feeling however, that now she was Queen it was something she could never do again.

She told herself that she was being needlessly apprehensive but she knew that while nobody would be shocked or surprised if the King joined with his people either dancing or celebrating it was something that would not be expected of their Queen.

"I am being pushed out of everything!"

She wanted to cry out at the injustice of it.

Suddenly she thought defiantly:

'I shall do what I want, and nobody shall stop me!'

But even to herself she did not sound very positive, and she had a feeling that it would be like the incident of her trousers which Vladilas had forbidden her to wear, and seeing the way he had treated her already, it would be impossible to defy him.

She stood at the window looking down at the lights and stamped her foot.

"Why did I not marry Tomilav when I had the chance?" she asked.

Then she thought of how Tomilav had left the room on Vladilas's order without even making the effort to say goodbye to her, or even look at her.

'He was frightened!' she thought comtemptuously.

She knew that fear and lack of confidence in himself would be something which she would despise in her husband.

Greta came bustling into the room.

"Your Majesty is awake!" she said. "I'll prepare your bath for you, and I expect His Majesty will be back soon."

"He is not yet here?" Ileana asked sharply.

"No, Your Majesty. He's still working down in the valley. I hears how he's making them all laugh. They say there has not been one grumble, not even from the older folk who're always ready to find fault."

"What is His Majesty doing?" Ileana asked.

She wanted to restrain herself from being too curious, but somehow she had to know.

"They say His Majesty's here, there and everywhere! The Gypsies are playing and singing, and the children have been paddling in the river. It's all like a wonderful picnic!"

There was a note of yearning in Greta's voice which tol Ileana she longed to be with them and she thought that was what she would like too.

But when Vladilas had left the Castle he had not suggested that she should join him.

Then insidiously, almost as if it was conjured up in front of her, she could see Thelia's lovely face and the expression in her eyes as she had looked at Vladilas as the wagon in which she was sitting drove into the valley.

Angry, because what she was thinking was like a

pain in her breast, Ileana said sharply:

"Hurry up about my bath, Greta! You are wasting time gossiping, which you know you are not supposed to do!"

She knew even as she spoke, that she was being unfair, but somehow she wanted to hurt somebody as she herself was feeling hurt because she was alone.

chapter seven

ILEANA lay in the darkness and knew that never in her whole life had she felt so lonely.

She had changed for dinner into a pretty gown which was white and thought as she did so that her father would have approved of her not wearing black.

"I hate gloomy-looking women," he had said after her mother died and had insisted that she wore white and mauve long before the conventional time for black was over.

"Now that I am Queen, I can do as I want," Ileana said aloud, but knew even as she spoke the words that they were untrue.

She knew she must do what the King wanted.

If not, he would be as angry with her as he had been when he found Prince Tomilav kissing her good-bye.

Yet when she was dressed she thought that even his critical eye could find no fault with her appearance.

She walked downstairs thinking she must find out exactly what he was doing and persuade him that to-morrow she should go with him and watch the work in the valley.

It was after eight o'clock when the Butler came to the Dining-Room where she was waiting, to say:

"I understand, Your Majesty, that His Majesty will not be returning for dinner."

"Why should you think that?" Ileana asked sharply.

"I hear, Your Majesty, there's been an accident of some kind, and His Majesty's sorting it out."

"His Majesty is not injured?"

"Oh, no, Your Majesty, and I am told it is nothing at all serious."

The last words made it impossible for Ileana to say she would go at once to the valley to see what had occurred.

Instead she knew that the only thing she could do was to stay where she was and hope that the King would be back later.

She ate dinner alone, as she had luncheon, waited on by what seemed to be a superfluous number of servants.

The food was excellent with, as far as she was concerned, too many dishes.

As soon as she could do so without it seeming unusual, she rose from the table saying:

"Come and inform me as soon as His Majesty returns. I shall be in the Drawing-Room."

As she walked along the passage with its attractive pictures and inlaid furniture, she felt that nothing could be more obvious than that the King had not wished her to come with him to the Castle.

Now he was behaving as if he was alone with no ties.

She thought it even more obvious when after waiting until nearly eleven o'clock she went upstairs, feeling by this time quite convinced that the King, having made the excuse of an accident, was now perhaps dancing with the Gypsies.

Thelia would be with him and this was the pattern their lives would take in the future.

"I cannot... bear it!" Ileana told herself, as Greta helped her to undress.

"I *will* not bear it!" she said aloud when she was alone in the darkness of her room.

She felt as if the future was like a long dark tunnel to which there was no end, and all she could see was darkness and despair.

She tried to think of how happy she had been before she had made the fatal mistake of climbing Bela to spy on the Pallikares and in consequence now found herself married to Vladilas.

There had been horses to ride, Cavalry Officers to accompany her, and because her father was unable to take charge her authority was accepted unquestioned.

'I ruled the country then,' she thought, 'but now nobody will listen to me, and Vladilas will have it all his own way!'

She told herself that she hated him even more fiercely than she had before, but she knew that was untrue.

In fact, she had a sneaking admiration for the way in which he had stepped into the seat of power with no opposition.

He would obviously as the year passed, become a hero figure with everybody admiring him for his strength and determination.

Because he was so handsome there would always

be women in his life, beautiful women like Thelia, with whom he would spend his leisure hours, and be concerned with his wife only on public occasions.

"It is intolerable! Absolutely intolerable!" Ileana said aloud.

But she felt as if her voice was lost and stifled in the beautiful room with the cupids over the bed and the silk curtains blotting out the stars.

Deep in the misery of her thoughts she must have dozed for some hours before she was awakened by what she thought had been a faint noise.

She was sure it was now well past the middle of the night and she wondered if she had awoken to the sound of a closing door and if it had been the King returning to his own room from the valley.

She had left one candle alight in the Sitting-Room which lay between their rooms and she could see the glimmer of it under the door.

It was the only light in the darkness and as she waited she knew that if it was the King he had not thought to come and tell her he was back.

"Why should he do so?" she asked. "He has never been near me ever since we married!"

She had to admit this was not surprising, considering the way she had behaved on their wedding-night when she had threatened him with his own knife.

And yet when she thought of it she could still feel the heaviness of his body on hers and the violence of his fingers clasping her wrist.

Even more insistent was the memory of his kisses

and the pain she had felt when his mouth had taken possession of hers.

Then there had followed that strange sensation which she could not describe, and yet was still so vivid that she could feel it happening again.

When he had released her he had walked away without looking back and had avoided her all that day and evening.

'I suppose he hates me as much as I hate him!' Ileana thought.

Somehow it was a very dismal idea, and she wondered if she could suggest to him that they call a truce and work together for the good of Zokāla.

He might with his weapons have frightened off their immediate enemies, but there would be others and inevitable problems of one sort or another in which she was sure two brains would be better than one.

As she wondered how she could persuade him that she was necessary, she clearly heard a strange noise.

At first it sounded like feet shuffling about, then she knew it came from overhead and it seemed to intensify.

She sat up in bed to listen, and as she did so she was almost certain that what she was hearing was people, perhaps walking on tip-toe or else very softly, but certainly moving about in the turret above her bedroom.

Suddenly she had visions of one of the neighbouring countries of Zokāla invading them, perhaps Rumania or Hungary.

As she thought of it she remembered that Vladilas had not brought any guns with him to the Mispa Valley, but had left them behind where they had been on display during the Funeral.

It would be a clever move for an enemy to come to Mispa where nobody would expect one and to occupy the Valley.

If that was what the enemy did, they could, in the same way Vladilas had invaded the Bela Valley, be ensconced with men and guns before the rest of Zokāla was aware of what had happened.

The noise overhead seemed to increase and Ileana thought she might be the only person who knew the danger of what was happening.

She jumped out of bed and without thinking she was clad only in a diaphanous nightgown, moved swiftly across the room towards the Sitting-Room and opened the door.

The candle was guttering low, but by its light it was easy for her to run to the opposite side of the room and open the door into Vladilas's bedroom.

Then as she did so she wondered what she would do if he was not there and how she would be able to inform him of what was going on in the turret.

But as she entered the room she saw that he was sitting up in bed with two lighted candles beside him reading some papers.

He looked up as she appeared and stared at her in astonishment.

Because she was frightened she said incoherently:

"There are...people...I am sure they are...enemies...they are climbing up into the turret...over my room...I can hear them...moving...it sounds as if there are a great number of them!"

For a moment Vladilas just went on looking at her. Then he said:

"I am sorry you have been disturbed. It is not people you are hearing in the turret, but bats."

As he finished the sentence Ileana gave a shrill scream and running towards him, flung herself against him.

"Save me!" she cried. "I...I cannot bear bats! They are terrifying! If...they get...caught in my hair...they can never get...free!"

Her words seemed to fall over themselves and were almost incoherent as she hid her face against his shoulder.

His arms went round her and she went on:

"Suppose they come...through the...ceiling? I cannot...bear it! They are...horried...like little devils...and they have...hooks on their wings!"

"It is all right," Vladilas said in his deep voice. "I will not let them hurt you."

"They...terrify me!" Ileana whispered.

His arms tightened.

"I promise you will be safe."

"I have...always been...frightened of...bats."

"I can understand that," he replied gently. "At the same time, it is unlike you to be afraid of anything, and I have always admired you for your bravery."

As he spoke quietly and kindly, for some reason she could not understand Ileana felt the tears come into her eyes.

"I . . . I am . . . not brave!" she stuttered. "I am . . . frightened of . . . bats . . . I am frightened of . . . being alone . . . and I am . . . frightened when you are . . . angry!"

As she spoke she felt the tears running down her cheeks.

Then quite suddenly she was shaking with a tempest of tears and weeping uncontrollably.

It was a culmination of the misery she had been feeling at being alone in the Castle, her fear of Vladilas's anger and his intention in the future to ignore her, except for when they appeared together in public.

She cried as a child might, forgetting where she was and who she clung to, only swept away by her own misery.

Vladilas held her very closely to him, moving her gently so that without her realising it she lay beside him in the bed, and he pulled the sheet over them both.

Then stroking her long hair with one hand he said gently:

"It is all right. There is nothing to make you afraid, and nothing to make you unhappy."

"B–but . . . I am alone . . . terribly alone!" Ileana sobbed. "You have Thelia and I know you . . . love her . . . but I have . . . nobody to love me . . . and I cannot . . . manage by . . . myself."

It was a confession she had never made before.

She heard the despair in her own voice and thought

she no longer had any pride and it did not matter if he knew the truth.

"My poor unhappy little wife," Vladilas said softly. "I see there is a lot of explaining to be done. Stop crying, and let me sweep away all the untrue things you are thinking. Tomorrow I will have the bats cleared from the turret and the place wired so that they can never return."

The calm way he spoke and the comfort of his arms around her made Ileana's tears abate a little.

She still kept her face hidden knowing she had made his silk nightshirt damp with the tempestuous way in which she had been crying.

But somehow the gentleness of his hand on her hair was very reassuring, and she knew while she was in his arms that the bats could not hurt her.

She had always been terrified of them ever since her Nurse told her a story of a bat being caught in a woman's hair, and it fluttered and fluttered until it became so entangled that the only way it could be freed was by cutting away all the hair.

Because of this story Ileana had always been frightened even to see a bat flying overhead when dusk came, or to hear their shrill whistle in the darkness.

Now in a very small voice she asked:

"Can you really...sweep them...away so that they...will not...come back?"

"I promise you they will all be removed tomorrow."

"B–but...I cannot...go back to that...room to-night!"

"No, of course not!" he said. "We will change rooms,

or you can stay here—with me."

It flashed through her mind that she could only feel safe when he was there, but she did not speak and after a moment he went on:

"I am sorry I could not come back in time for dinner tonight, but there was an accident to one of the men as he was unloading a wagon. His leg was very badly gashed, and because we thought it was broken I had to fetch a doctor from the City to attend him."

He paused before he said:

"I can only blame myself for not having brought a doctor with me in the first place. I had actually arranged for one to arrive as soon as we had built a hut which could be used, if necessary, as a Hospital."

Ileana did not speak and after a moment he continued:

"When that was done, and I had found somebody to look after his wife and family for the night, it was too late to come back to dine with you. I therefore accepted something to eat from one of the women who had travelled with me when I first arrived and who is an excellent cook."

He smiled before he went on:

"You will understand that as I had eaten nothing since breakfast, I was in fact very hungry."

Ileana was listening, but she had not raised her head from his shoulder. Now she felt him draw her a little closer to him and he said:

"I did not stay with Thelia, because she was with her husband."

"Her . . . husband!"

Ileana was not certain whether she said the words aloud or merely murmured them in her mind.

"Thelia is married to one of my most trusted Lieutenants who will be in charge of the Mispa Valley," Vladilas explained. "They were both very anxious to come here and build their own house, because Thelia is expecting a baby."

Ileana drew in her breath.

"B–but . . . she loves you!"

"I think she has always had a kind of hero-worship for me," Vladilas replied. "I have known her ever since she was a child. Her family are Greek and were friends of my mother's."

"She is . . . very beautiful," Ileana murmured, "and . . . I thought you . . . loved her."

"She is very beautiful," Vladilas agreed, "and I might perhaps have fallen in love with her two years ago when she was eighteen, but I was already very much in love with somebody else."

Ileana stiffened.

"So you were . . . in love!" she said in a low voice.

"Yes, I was in love," Vladilas agreed, "and I found it difficult to find any other woman as beautiful, or in fact to think of anybody else."

There was a short silence. Then he went on:

"Then when I saw for the second time, the woman I loved six months ago, I knew she was everything I admired and wanted in my wife."

Ileana drew in her breath.

Now she would definitely have moved away from Vladilas, but his arms imprisoned her.

"Why . . . did you not . . . marry her?" she demanded.

She knew as she spoke that is was impossible to hide what was a note of despair in her voice.

"I did!" Vladilas said quietly.

For a moment Ileana felt she could not have heard him aright, and she raised her head to look up at him.

"Did you say . . . you . . . m—married her?"

"I married her!"

"B—but . . . you said you had fallen in love . . . two years ago!"

"That was when I first saw you. I came to Zokāla to spy out the land, to see what had happened to my father's Castle and to discover if the country to which I really belonged was as attractive as it had always sounded."

"Then what happened?"

"I saw a girl who was so beautiful, so exquisite, that I felt she could not be real, but must have stepped down from the snow-covered mountains!"

Ileana made an inarticulate little sound and once again her face was against him as he went on:

"You were riding superbly with an expertise that I admired but I knew it was not what you did, but what you were that mattered."

"Why did I not . . . know you were . . . there?"

"Why should you?" Vladilas replied. "I was just an ordinary traveller passing through the country, but inquisitive enough to learn a great deal from the people whom I talked to about their Princess."

"But . . . you did not try to . . . meet me?"

"I was not quite certain how your father would receive me, and I had always resented the way he had driven my father into exile."

"But... after you left you... thought about me?"

"I found it impossible to think of anything else," Vladilas answered. "Then after my father's death, and when I heard that the King was in a coma, I came back, having visited Austria and Hungary and learnt their intentions with regard to Zokāla."

"What happened after... that?"

"I knew when I saw you," he said quietly, "that I would never rest until you belonged to me!"

Ileana raised her head again.

"You... wanted me?"

"Shall I tell you how much?" he asked very quietly.

Then as he looked down at her tear-streaked face, her long eyelashes which were wet, and her lips trembling with the emotion she had passed through he pulled her against him and his mouth came down on hers.

He kissed her possessively, determinedly, and at the same time with a tenderness he had never shown before.

Ileana knew this was what she had been wanting and longing for, even though she was not aware of it.

Incredibly the sensations he aroused in her were a rapture that swept through her, rising through her breasts into her throat, then to her lips.

It was a strange ecstasy that was like nothing she had ever imagined, but was part of herself and part of Vladilas as well.

She could feel his heart beating against hers and she knew strangely, unexpectedly, that she loved him, and had loved him for a long time.

Although she had refused to admit it to herself she had loved the mastery of him, the manner in which he had married her by force, even as he had lifted her by force from her horse onto his.

It was what she admired in a man, wanted in her husband, and only her pride and spirit of independence had made her fight against him.

And yet, instinctively, she had known it was hopeless and because he wanted her, she was his.

He kissed her until Ileana felt as if she was joined to him so completely and so absolutely that they were no longer two people but one.

Then as he seemed to draw her closer and still closer she felt as if he was carrying her up to the very peaks of the mountains and beyond.

Her whole body seemed to pulsate with the magnetism that came from him, and yet was a part of herself.

Now his hand was touching her, and his lips were becoming more insistent, more demanding, and yet she was not afraid.

She felt as if he was asking something of her and she wanted to give it to him, even while she did not know what it was.

As he kissed her and went on kissing her she had the feeling that he drew both her heart and her soul from her body, and yet was asking more.

Only when he raised his head did she say with a

rapt note in her voice he had never heard before:

"I love you...oh, Vladilas...I...love you!"

"As I love you, my precious darling!"

As he turned round and laid her against the pillows so that he could look down at her, she was afraid that she might lose him and her arms went out towards him.

"I...I love you!" she said again. "Please...do not leave me."

"Do you think that possible?"

Then he was kissing her wildly, passionately, and she felt his lips on her neck, her shoulders, her breasts, arousing new feelings she did not even know existed.

Now they were no longer touching the peaks of the mountains but the stars above them, and as Vladilas drew her closer still Ileana knew that they were no longer human but one with the gods.

*   *   *

A long time later when the candles beside the bed were guttering low Ileana stirred in Vladilas's arms and asked:

"Do you...still love me?"

"My precious," he replied, "that is the question I should be asking you."

"I...I did not...know that love could be so...wonderful...so glorious!" she whispered.

"I made you happy? I did not hurt you?"

"It was...perfect!"

"And you are no longer frightened of me?"

"I should be very...very frightened if you did not...love me...and left me alone...as you did today."

"I will never do that."

"After you were...angry with me...because I was with...Tomilav...you did not speak to me...or look at me."

"If I had I would have swept you into my arms and not only kissed you, but made you mine."

"I know now that it would have been...very marvellous...but I did not understand."

"What did you not understand?"

"That making love is so...thrilling...so glorious like the sunshine...the flowers and climbing to the top of the...mountains!"

"My darling, that is what I wanted you to feel."

"Did you...feel like...that?"

"Loving you was the supreme moment of my life."

"Oh, Vladilas...I love you!"

"And I love you, my beautiful wife! But Prince Tomilav was fortunate to leave the Palace without having his nose broken!"

"I was only going to let him...kiss my cheek!"

Vladilas's arms encircled her like bars of steel.

"Let me make this clear, my adorable one," he said. "I am a Brigand and if any man touches you, except respectfully, I swear I will murder him, and beat you!"

Ileana gave a little gurgle of laughter.

"It is exciting to think I can make you jealous when I have been so desperately jealous of Thelia...and I expected because I thought you did not...love me that there would be dozens of Thelias in the future to make me...unhappy."

"I will not even know another woman exists unless you cease to love me," Vladilas replied. "I know now you are what I always wanted, but thought I should never find."

There was silence for a moment. Then Ileana said:

"I cannot understand quite why you...love me when whatever you may say I am not the...soft... gentle...obedient woman you...want as your... wife."

Vladilas's lips were very near to hers as he said:

"You are quite certain that is what you will not be in the future?"

"Is that what you are going to bully me into being?"

"Not bully you, my precious, just love you."

He smoothed her hair away from her forehead before he said:

"I adore your beauty and love your quick, intelligent little brain, but what I want in a woman is somebody who, when she is with me, is as you say very soft, gentle and feminine."

Because of the way he spoke Ileana felt her whole being respond to him, and yet some little flicker of independence within her made her say provocatively:

"And if you...cannot immediately get your own...way, I presume you will force me into...doing what you...want!"

"I forced you into marriage because we were pressed for time," Vladilas replied, "but I did not force you to come to me tonight, In fact, I was expecting to lie sleepless, wanting you, but determined not to come to your room, as I longed to do."

Ileana looked up at him.

Then she said:

"What I think you are saying is that you were fighting me in a rather . . . crafty manner. Is that the truth?"

"Perhaps," Vladilas admitted.

"You were attacking the enemy skilfully and subtly," Ileana went on, "but at the same time you could not have known that the bats would play a leading part in your offensive."

"If it had not been the bats it would have been something else," Vladilas said. "But I knew eventually you would be mine, as I wanted you to be."

"In simple words . . . I surrendered!"

"Exactly!" he agreed. "That, my darling, is what you did, but I did not mean to make you cry."

"And yet, because I was . . . frightened, and because you . . . made me so . . . unhappy it was very . . . feminine."

"Very feminine," Vladilas agreed, "and very adorable, but I promise I will try in the future never to make you cry again, even if it has given me what I wanted!"

She looked up at him enquiringly, and he explained:

"A woman I can protect and comfort: a woman who turns to me because she needs me, as a man."

Ileana looked shy for a moment before she said:

"Perhaps if I am always complacent and clinging you will be . . . bored with me."

Vladilas smiled.

"I adore your clinging to me."

"And if I do...not?"

"Then I may leave you alone with the bats!"

Ileana gave a little scream and held onto him.

"How can you...think of anything so cruel...so wicked?"

Vladilas looked at her very tenderly.

"I am only making sure, my sweet, that you cling to me and need me."

"Oh, darling, I do!" she whispered. "I need you...desperately...I need your love...I want to be...with you!"

"You can be quite certain of that! We shall be together both by day and by night, and I promise you that I will never allow you to be frightened and there will certainly be no other men kissing you behind my back!"

Ileana laughed.

"I have no wish for...anybody to...kiss me except...you...You are so wonderful!"

"Can you really be saying that to me?" Vladilas asked.

Ileana laughed again.

"It is rather surprising," she admitted, "but every time I look at you, every time I think about you, and every time you touch me, I find you so wonderful that there are no words to express what I feel..."

She put up her arm as she spoke and pulled his head down to hers.

"I have never been in love before," she murmured, "and I want you to...teach me what I should say...and what I should do...to make you love me."

Vladilas drew in his breath.

"That is very easy," he answered. "All you have to do is to give me yourself, completely and absolutely. I want your thoughts, your ideas, your feelings, and of course, my precious love, your beautiful, exquisite body."

His hand was touching her again and Ileana felt herself quiver.

The thought flashed through her mind that it would be wonderful if he gave her a son who looked like him.

The future was no longer dark and frightening, but brilliant with colour, and a thousand unthought-of possibilities which all concerned Vladilas and love!

"It is . . . all so . . . exciting!" she said rapturously.

"I want to excite you, my beautiful wife," he replied, "and now I can see what I longed for when I thought despairingly it would never happen."

"What is that?" she asked curiously.

"That the fire in your green eyes is not the fire of hatred, but love!"

The way he spoke made Ileana feel the fire leap with her breasts and she said:

"When you touch me . . . and when you . . . make love to me . . . I feel there is not only fire in my eyes but that . . . the flames are . . . running through my body it is . . . very . . . thrilling, very exciting, and something that has never . . . happened to me before."

She knew that what she said excited Vladilas, for now she saw a fire in his eyes.

Then he was kissing her again, kissing her as if he

wooed her, and at the same time was determined to dominate her.

She knew he was asking her to surrender herself to him completely and absolutely, and there was nothing else in the world except him.

She knew as they drew closer and closer to each other that that was what the future held.

A love so tremendous, so overwhelming, that it not only made them complete in themselves, but through it they could create a country of beauty, peace and prosperity for all those who followed them.

Then as Vladilas made her his there was only the love which is Life itself, and Heaven too.

Barbara Cartland, the world's most famous romantic novelist, who is also an historian, playwright, lecturer, political speaker and television personality, has now written over 370 books and sold over 370 million books over the world.

She has also had many historical works published and has written four autobiographies as well as the biographies of her mother and that of her brother, Ronald Cartland, who was the first Member of Parliament to be killed in the last war. This book has a preface by Sir Winston Churchill and has just been republished with an introduction by Sir Arthur Bryant.

Love at the Helm, a novel written with the help and inspiration of the late Admiral of the Fleet, the Earl Mountbatten of Burma, is being sold for the Mountbatten Memorial Trust.

Miss Cartland in 1978 sang an Album of Love Songs with the Royal Philharmonic Orchestra.

In 1976 by writing twenty-one books, she broke

the world record and has continued for the following six years with twenty-four, twenty, twenty-three, twenty-four, twenty-four, and twenty-five. She is in the *Guinness Book of Records* as the best-selling author in the world.

She is unique in that she was one and two in the Dalton List of Best Sellers, and one week had four books in the top twenty.

In private life Barbara Cartland, who is a Dame of the Order of St. John of Jerusalem, Chairman of the St. John Council in Hertfordshire and Deputy President of the St. John Ambulance Brigade, has also fought for better conditions and salaries for Midwives and Nurses.

Barbara Cartland is deeply interested in Vitamin Therapy and is President of the British National Association for Health. Her book *The Magic of Honey* has sold throughout the world and is translated into many languages. Her designs "Decorating with Love" are being sold all over the USA, and the National Home Fashions League named her, in 1981, "Woman of Achievement."

Barbara Cartland's Romances (a book of cartoons) has recently been published in Great Britain and the U.S.A., as well as a cookery book, *The Romance of Food*.

____	06297-9	LIGHT OF THE GODS #6	$1.95
____	07308-3	BRIDE TO A BRIGAND #7	$2.50
____	07607-4	LOVE COMES WEST #8	$2.50

Prices may be slightly higher in Canada.